STAMPEDE RUSTLERS?

"What you said about these jaspers," Curly interjected, addressing Gabe. "It's all true?"

"What reason would I have to lie about a thing like this?"

"He's probably just trying to cover up the fact that him and the rest of you drovers couldn't keep your beeves under control," Charley suggested contemptuously.

Dillworth muttered an obscenity. Then, speaking slowly, his anger obviously on the verge of bursting forth, he added, "I believe what he says. You boys better get out of here before I lose my temper and get you out."

Curly exploded into a string of shouted curses and sprang at Bud. . . .

SPECIAL PREVIEW!

Turn to the back of this book for a sneak-peek excerpt of the new epic western series . . .

THE HORSEMEN

. . . the sprawling, unforgettable story of a family of horse breeders and trainers—from the Civil War South to the wild West.

Also in the LONG RIDER Series

LONG RIDER

★ CHISHOLM TRAIL ★

CLAY DAWSON

DIAMOND BOOKS, NEW YORK

CHAPTER ONE

He rode through the forest of blackjack oaks in almost total silence. He moved like a shadow among other shadows, blending in with his surroundings, a man hard to notice unless he wanted to be noticed.

His shirt was tan, the color of the soil his horse trod. His flat-topped black Stetson was unadorned except for a thin leather band encircling its crown. His Frisco jeans were faded and worn, and his army boots were scarred and unpolished. The bandanna tied around his neck was a shade darker than his shirt.

The buckskin he rode was big-barreled and strong-shouldered. It responded readily to the pressure of its rider's knees and the man's hands on the reins. Horse and man seemed to be one creature, so smoothly did they move together, the rider swaying slightly in the saddle as he shifted his weight and the horse moving easily and alertly through the sun-dappled woods.

The rider's name was Gabe Conrad. Because he had been raised among the Oglala Sioux until he was fourteen years old, his name—given him by the Indians among whom he grew up—was also Long Rider. The latter name had been bestowed upon him in his fourteenth year after he rode many miles through a blizzard to warn a Sioux village of a planned raid by the United States Army. Two horses had died under him during that long and grueling ride which, it had seemed to him at the time, would never end. But end it did and because of it and him many Sioux lives were saved.

Long Rider.

The name was a tribute from a grateful people. An honor he humbly accepted. One he secretly took great pride in.

His face was one not easily forgotten—especially by women. Perhaps that fact was due to the penetrating quality of his clear gray eyes which seemed to pierce whatever they looked at. Or perhaps it was due to the complicated geometry of the planes and angles that composed the features of his face. A thin nose. Sunken cheeks below sharp cheekbones. Square chin beneath the parallel lines of his thin lips.

His hair was the soft color of sand. It covered the collar of his shirt and hid his ears from sight.

He glanced up at the sky. By the position of the sun, he knew it was nearly noon. By the grumbling in his gut, he knew he was more than hungry; he was ravenous. He hadn't eaten since the night before and then only some roasted sego lily bulbs he had dug. It was time to hunt.

But, before he could put that thought into appropriate action, he spotted a silver glimmer in the distance as he emerged from the woods—a silver glimmer caused by the sun's light reflecting off the surface of a stream. With a tug on the reins and slight knee pressure, he turned his buckskin to the right and headed for the stream.

Along the way, he stopped long enough to gather some devil's shoestring and buckeye.

When he reached the stream, he dismounted and walked along the bank until he found what he was looking for: a deep hole in the stream's bottom. Into it, he cast the leaves of the plants he had kneaded into a pulp. Then he hunkered down on the bank to wait, his eyes on the spot where he had placed the plants.

Many minutes went by during which the sun passed its meridian. Gabe waited impatiently, resisting the absurd urge to wade into the water and try to catch a fish to eat.

"Patience makes the difference between one who tries and one who succeeds."

The words, spoken long ago to Gabe by a shaman, a holy man of the People, as the Oglala called themselves, echoed in his mind. He had never forgotten them, and they came to him now out of the distant past to calm him as he waited for the catch that would, in good time, be his.

Iron Horse was the name of the shaman who had taught young Gabe the many things he needed to know to survive in the wild and the wider world. It was Iron Horse who had taught him how to read the spiders' webs to know when rain was coming. How to peel the bark of the yellow pine and eat its inner surface when no other nourishment was to be had. How to make snowshoes of willow wood and rawhide which would allow their wearer to hunt the rabbits wearing their white winter coats no matter how deep snow lay upon the land.

It was Iron Horse who had taught Gabe about the world beyond the world. Iron Horse had told him the stories of *Skan* the Sky which was the source of all power and who provided each man with a Spirit or personality, a Ghost or vitality, a Spirit-like essence, and a Potency or power. Skan, said old Iron Horse, would judge a man's Spirit at the time of his death upon the testimony of the man's Ghost.

For long hours Iron Horse told the wide-eyed young Gabe vivid stories of the People's Associate Gods—*Whope,* the Beautiful One, defender of chastity; *Hanwi,* the Moon; and *Tate,* the Wind, guardian of the Spirit Trail, which white men called the Milky Way, who admitted to the world beyond the world those whom Skan had judged worthy.

A *Wicasa Wakan* was Iron Horse, Gabe thought. A true holy man.

A faint plop shattered his fond reverie.

He became conscious again of the surface of the water he had been so intently watching. On it rested two catfish, a full-grown one and a smaller one. He reached down and seized them both.

They lay limply in his hands, the larger one twitching its tail but otherwise dormant. The drug Gabe had placed in the water—the soporific combination of buckeye and devil's shoestring, an old Indian way of catching fish— had done its job.

He drew his knife and slit open both fish. After gutting the fish, Gabe washed what remained of the carcasses in the cool water of the stream. He used his knife to scrape the scales from the fish, working from the tails toward the heads. The smaller fish shed its scales readily but the more mature fish seemed at first to resist Gabe's attempts to scale it.

When he had completed his task, he placed the scaled and gutted fish in the shallow water of the stream to cool and went in search of wood. He found a rotting deadfall in the woods and gathered up enough of it to build a small fire. When he had his fire going, he removed the larger fish from the shallows. Leaving the skin on it, he split it in half and placed it skin side down on a flat stone. He repeated the process with the second smaller fish. He propped the stone up and then hunkered down to wait for the fillets to bake.

Some time later, when the fish were baked through, he speared one of the fillets with a twig and proceeded to devour it, burning his tongue in the process. He continued eating with little or no regard to the way the fillets were scorching his mouth because of his intense hunger.

Within minutes all four fillets had disappeared. Gabe washed the last of them down with water he took from the stream in his cupped hands. Then he filled his canteen, stamped out his fire, and tightened his cinch strap before resuming his journey.

He had not been riding long when he came to a spot where the Chisholm Trail joined his own. He rode out onto the Chisholm, following it north. It was a wide trail that had been trampled down by cattle in places to a width of between two and four hundred yards. It had also been cut by years of erosion so that it lay well below the level of the plains it crossed. As Gabe followed it, he occasionally passed the stark white bones of cattle killed in stampedes and those of calves that had been shot at birth because they could not keep up with the drives. There were other bones too but not visible ones. Only weatherworn wooden crosses marked the spots where the forgotten bones of long-dead cowhands lay interred in shallow graves, victims of one mishap or another on their drives. The cowhands' graves reminded Gabe of something he had once heard a drover say in a saloon in Abilene, Kansas:

"The cowhands on a drive are worth a helluva lot less than the cows they drive. My motto on a drive is this: look out for the cows' feet and the horses' backs and let the cowhands and the cook take care of themselves."

Gabe's buckskin picked its way carefully along the rutted trail which was almost totally devoid of grass or undergrowth of any kind. It was a dry path redolent of dust and the rotting manure of the many head of cattle which had passed over it. On either side of the trail, grass grew tall enough to reach a rider's knees and polish his boots were he to ride through it. In spots it had been trampled by cattle that had strayed and been pursued by mounted cowboys.

As he rode up a rise, Gabe pulled his hat down low on his forehead to cut the glare of the sun that was turning the summer landscape into a furnace.

As he topped the rise, he saw a herd in the distance. Longhorns, almost all of them, although there were examples of a few other breeds as well among the drift. They were heading north along the Trail, their horns swinging as they lumbered along. Close to three hundred head, Gabe estimated. The drovers numbered six in addition to the trail boss riding in front of the herd. All of them were being kept busy riding out after strays and keeping the drift in line.

One cowboy, to Gabe's amusement, had his hands full as he tried to round up a single cow which seemed determined to retrace its steps. The cow ran to the right. When the cowboy wheeled his horse and went after her, she turned on a dime despite her great bulk and headed to the left. The cowboy brought his horse to a halt, turned it, and rode after the recalcitrant cow.

The animal deftly evaded him. Even when the cowboy used his coiled lariat to try to whip her into submission, she continued to run in an apparently haphazard course, giving him and his mount a run for their money.

Gabe grinned as the faint echo of the cowboy's cursing and the cow's bawling reached his ears, borne as they were by a rising wind from the north. It wasn't until the cow reached the drag that she slowed her pace. In she went among the orphans and the cripples and the just plain trail-dawdlers. Minutes later, she was placidly moving ahead with the drift, having taken her place in the drag beside a calf which was apparently hers and from which she just as apparently had become separated during the journey. Both cow and calf plodded along to the tune of the frustrated cursing of the cowboy who had been pursuing the cow. He turned his mount and rode out of the thick cloud of dust the drag was raising which was causing the two men riding behind the herd to cough through the protective bandannas they had bound around their faces to cover their noses and mouth.

On the left side of the herd the wrangler moved his remuda along at a steady pace. Ahead of him and just behind the man riding point, the chuck wagon rattled and rumbled along, the cook driving it.

As the leaders of the herd began to round a bend up ahead of them to avoid a series of uneven hummocks rising from the prairie, Gabe was about to put heels to his mount and head down from the rise. But he hesitated when he saw three riders heading west toward the herd from behind the hummocks. All of them, he noted, were armed. They were approaching the herd at a right angle, the hummocks separating them from it.

Gabe sat his saddle, watching as the three men stopped on the eastern side of the cluster of hummocks and conferred briefly. He continued to watch as one of the three men took something from a gunnysack tied to his saddle horn and started up toward the crest of the tallest hummock.

It took Gabe a minute or two to be able to make out what the man had in his hand. It was a chicken. Now what, he wondered, is that fellow going to do with that Rhode Island Red? Sell it to the drive's cook? Roast and eat it himself?

As the mounted man neared the top of the hummock, he drew rein and dismounted. Gabe watched him drop to his hands and knees and, still clutching the chicken by the legs, crawl up to the hummock's crest.

The man waited until the swing man on the eastern side of the herd was busily engaged in chasing a pair of steers which had left the drift and were challenging one another, their dangerous horns aimed at each other's heads. The man on the hummock chose that moment to throw the chicken in his hand down into the midst of the herd just behind the spot where the point man was riding.

The chicken, loudly cackling its fright, its wings flapping wildly, some of its feathers tearing loose from its body and drifting away on the wind, landed on the back of one of the steers and then disappeared in the mass of moving bodies.

The steer that had been struck by the careening chicken let out a loud bawl and lunged forward, knocking the steer directly ahead of it to its knees. It, in turn, caused the cattle on either side of it to bolt to the right and left.

The cowboys began to shout to one another as the cattle in their charge broke from the drift as if it were a cake suddenly crumbling. Despite the best efforts of the drovers, the cattle fled in all directions as their rout swiftly became a full-fledged stampede.

The stampede split into three main branches, one heading north, one heading west, and one turning south toward the rise on which Gabe sat aboard his buckskin. Shouts from the cowboys filled the air. Shouts and colorful curses. But the cattle, as in every stampede, were silent. Only the pounding of their hooves bore thunderous testimony to the awesome reality of their headlong flight.

Gabe spurred his mount into movement when he saw one of the two cowboys who were desperately trying to turn the southern-bound cattle get himself in the terrifying position of being pursued by the racing animals as they, for no apparent reason, suddenly swerved and headed in his direction.

Gabe rode down the rise at a heart-stopping gallop. As he did so, the fleeing cowboy looked back over his shoulder and let out a strangled cry that was more scream than anything else. The man's legs pumped wildly as he repeatedly spurred his horse in a frantic attempt to outrun the cattle closing in behind him.

Gabe narrowed the distance between himself and the man and as he did so, the cowboy turned in his saddle and fired his side arm into the faces of the oncoming cattle.

One of the steers went down, blood spurting from its shattered skull. The cattle immediately behind it stumbled over its body and also went down. One of them, when it rose, immediately fell again, its right front leg broken and unable to support its weight. That animal died beneath the iron-hard hooves of the other cattle behind it which ran relentlessly over the fallen creature.

Gabe closed in on the man fleeing the stampede. As he did so, he ripped his slicker free of the piggin' string that bound it behind the cantle of his saddle. Holding the yellow garment in his right hand, he rode at a rapid pace toward the steer that was leading the stampede. When he got close enough to it, he flailed at the animal with his slicker in an attempt to turn it. Although the longhorn shied away from the slashing slicker, it did not turn but instead continued to race onward.

Gabe, leaning to the right, flailed again and again at the steer, striking it on the head, surprised that he had not blinded it by his furious actions. Still the steer did not turn.

A scream from the cowboy riding ahead of the mass of bodies that were giving off intense heat as a result of their exertions caused Gabe to turn his head. What he saw horrified him. The cowboy's horse had stumbled when its foot went down into a gopher hole, and the cowboy had gone sailing over the animal's head. He hit the ground with a resounding thud that could be heard above the noise of the oncoming herd.

Gabe wasted no time. He spurred his buckskin, and the animal responded with a new burst of speed which took Gabe away from the lead steer he had not been able to stop, let alone turn, and toward the cowboy who, with a terror-stricken expression on his face, had scrambled to his feet and was running ahead of the herd.

Throwing his slicker over the withers of his horse, Gabe headed for the man. A glance over his shoulder as he continued riding hell-for-leather revealed that the steers had been slowed somewhat by the body of the cowboy's mount in their path.

The horse screamed, a sound that was cut off in mid-cry as the steers trampled it to death.

Gabe leaned down and held out his hand. The cowboy reached out for it—but missed. As Gabe's momentum carried him forward, the cowboy increased his pace, and this time when Gabe held out his hand, the man managed to catch hold of it. With a mighty pull, Gabe lifted him off the ground. A moment later, the cowboy was seated somewhat precariously behind him, his arms wrapped around Gabe's waist as he held on tightly, his breath hot on the back of Gabe's neck as he wordlessly sobbed his terror into the air.

Gabe wheeled his buckskin so hard the bit cut into the tender flesh of the horse's mouth and drew blood which blended with the saliva that was flying from the animal's mouth, turning it into a pink spray.

Gabe slowed his mount once he was safely out of the path of the racing steers. He drew rein and sat his saddle, watching as the longhorns went pounding past him and the man he had managed to rescue in the very nick of time.

"Sweet bleeding Jesus!" sobbed the cowboy behind him. "I thought I was a goner for sure and certain. Mister, you came out of the blue like you was my guardian angel, and I'm in your debt for life for keeping me from turning into mincemeat under those ornery beasts' killer feet!"

"You just had yourself a close call, there's not a doubt about that."

The cowboy slid down over the rump of Gabe's buckskin and wiped the sweat from his face with the back of his hand. "I'm mighty obliged to you, mister. You saved my life is what you went and did." He held up his hand.

Gabe shook it.

"My name's McLean. Jonas McLean, only everybody calls me Curly."

"Gabe Conrad."

Curly gazed off into the distance where the dust was settling after the passage of the cattle that had stampeded in that direction. "It's going to take us a while to round up all those damn fool steers. We'll lose a few days in the doing of it too, or I miss my guess." He pushed his hat back on his head. "We've been on the trail now for close to a month. It begins to look to me like we ain't never going to get to Dodge City."

"I'll be moving on," Gabe told the man. "Good luck to you."

"Hey, mister, don't go yet," Curly cried. "I want you to meet our trail boss. His name's Dillworth. He'll be happy to hear about how you saved my life. Come on."

As Curly started on foot for the spot where the other drovers were rounding up a few head of cattle that had stopped stampeding and had begun to mill, Gabe shrugged and thought, Why not? He rode out after Curly.

"Hey, there, Mr. Dillworth!" Curly shouted as he neared the trail boss who was aboard his horse and shouting orders to his drovers. "I got me a hero you'll be pleased to meet up with!" Curly turned and pointed to Gabe. "That there's the man who just saved my life, Mr. Dillworth," he crowed. "What happened was . . ."

Gabe drew rein and sat his saddle in silence while Curly gave Dillworth a brief description of what had just happened.

Dillworth, when Curly had finished his tale, turned his sharp green eyes on Gabe. "I'm obliged to you," he said, offering his hand to Gabe. "You didn't have to do what you did."

"I don't agree with you there," Gabe said as he shook hands with the trail boss. "The way I saw it, I did have to do what I did. If I didn't—well—"

"If he didn't, I'd be deader'n a doornail and that's a true fact," Curly declared solemnly before beginning to grin and adding, "Mr. Dillworth, the real reason I wanted him to meet you—he says his name's Gabe Conrad, by the way—is that I reckoned you might maybe want to hire him to take Slim's place."

Dillworth's eyes, which were still on Gabe, never wavered. "I fired the man Curly's referring to," he said, "for sleeping on watch. So we're short a man on this drive. From what Curly has just told me about you, Conrad, you sound like the kind of man any trail boss would be glad to have in his crew. You want a job?"

Did he? Gabe wasn't sure. In fact, Dillworth's offer had taken him by surprise.

"Forty a month and found," Dillworth said, each word clipped short as he spoke. "I grant you a cattle drive's a hard way to earn that kind of money. But the job's there if you want to take it."

Gabe was aware of Curly watching him almost as intently as was Dillworth. He considered the offer briefly and then, with a nod, said, "I'll take it."

"I'm going to stick to him like a flea on a bluetick hound," Curly exclaimed. "In case there's another stampede, I mean," he added, his grin returning. "Considering the way he got me out of harm's way, I reckon Conrad could pluck a damned soul right out of Lucifer's own hot and horny hands."

At that moment, a drover rode up and drew rein beside Dillworth. "I counted twelve head dead, Boss. We've rounded up about a third of the herd, and the boys are out hunting the rest. It's going to take us one helluva long time to find them and bring them back here where they belong."

"Well, we'd best all get to it," Dillworth declared. "Oh, by the way, this new fellow is joining us, Dave. His name's Gabe Conrad. He lent a hand to Curly during the fracas."

"He saved my life is what he did, Dave," Curly declared.

"Meet Dave Carmody," Dillworth said to Gabe.

"Howdy." Gabe received no response from Carmody other than a stony stare.

The man was burly and built like a barrel. He stood only a few inches over five feet. He had shoulders almost as wide as a barn door. His blunt-fingered hands were strong, and he looked to Gabe as if he could fight a bear with a switch. The man's black eyes were as cold as Christmas, and his lips looked as if they might never have learned how to smile.

"Conrad, you ride with Curly," Dillworth ordered. "Head north after the beeves that went that way. Dave, you—"

Whatever order Dillworth had been about to give Carmody was interrupted by the appearance of three men who came riding down from the top of the tallest hummock that loomed in the near distance toward Dillworth and the men with him.

"The trail boss around?" one of the men asked as they rode up and drew rein.

"You're looking at him," Dillworth said. "What can I do for you gents?"

"Looks like you had some trouble here," one of the other two men remarked.

"Bad trouble," said the third man laconically. "Stampede trouble!"

"We heard it as we were heading this way, and then we saw it," the first man said. "We came to offer you some help."

"Help?" Dillworth asked, frowning.

"That's right. We'll be happy to help you round up those beeves that took off on you like they thought they'd turned into big birds." The leader of the group grinned at Dillworth. "For a dollar a head."

The trail boss shook his head. "I work on a tight budget. The owners of the cattle I'm driving to Dodge, they hired me and my men on the cheap. I got no cash to spare."

"It'll take you days to find every steer that ran off on you," one of the men observed. "Our price, it's not only fair, it's a bargain."

"I appreciate your offer to help," Dillworth said, "but I can't accept it. Me and my men'll have to do the job for ourselves. Like I just told you, we're operating on the thin line between have and have not. Why, our cook went and ran out of salt day before yesterday, and we used the last of our lump jaw cattle cure the day before that, and we've got no extra money to buy any more of either one.

"But it's good of you boys to offer to help us out of a tough spot. I'm just sorry I can't pay you for the help you're offering."

"My name's Bud," the leader of the three men volunteered. "This here"—he pointed to the man on his right—"he's Charley, and this here"—he pointed to the man on his left—"he's Duke. Maybe we can come to some kind of arrangement that'll satisfy everybody concerned."

"I told you—" Dillworth began but got no farther.

He was interrupted by Bud who said, "We'll help you with the roundup for just six bits a head, how's that strike you?"

"Six bits," Dillworth said, "might as well be six dollars. I told you this outfit's about one step away from being busted."

Bud glanced first at Duke and then at Charley. Both men nodded at him. He turned back to Dillworth and said, "Four bits."

Dillworth hesitated. "Fifty cents a head, you say?"

"Our best offer," Bud said firmly.

"Well—"

"Wait a minute, Dillworth," Gabe interjected.

"Four bits," Dillworth said, "isn't a bad offer. With the help of these three men, we can maybe save a day or two. Time's money, Conrad."

"That fellow there," Gabe said, pointing at Bud, "is the one who started the stampede."

"He what?" Dillworth asked, incredulity in his eyes.

"You heard me. I saw him from up on top of that rise back there. I saw him and Charley and Duke ride west toward those hummocks. Then I saw Bud dismount and take a chicken out of a gunnysack he was carrying. He climbed up to the top of the hummock, waited for the right moment, and when he decided it was at hand, he threw the chicken down into the herd. It scared the steer it hit, and that's what started the stampede."

Dillworth glanced from Gabe to Bud. "Is what he said true?"

"If it is," Carmody put in angrily, "I'll kill all three of those bastards with my own bare hands!"

"True?" Bud echoed. "Of course it's not true. That man's lying."

"I'm not lying," Gabe said, "and you know I'm not. I saw what I said I saw. You started the stampede so you and your friends could ride in and offer your services in rounding up the cattle you sent on their merry way for whatever amount of money you could gouge out of Mr. Dillworth."

"What you said about these jaspers," Curly interjected, addressing Gabe. "It's all true?"

"It's all true. What reason would I have to lie about a thing like this?"

"He's probably just trying to cover up the fact that him and the rest of you drovers couldn't keep your beeves under control," Charley suggested contemptuously.

Dillworth muttered an obscenity. Then, speaking slowly, his anger obviously on the verge of bursting forth, added, "This man"—he indicated Gabe—"wasn't on the drive with us when the stampede started. I believe what he says. There wasn't any reason for my cattle to stampede. No thunder. No lightning. No nothing. You boys better get out of here before I lose my temper and get you out."

Curly exploded into a string of shouted curses and sprang at Bud. "You—what you and your friends did cost me a good horse! The best horse I ever had! A horse that wasn't just a horse but a *friend*, goddammit!" He grabbed Bud's right leg and jerked him out of the saddle.

Bud hit the ground with a thud, and then Curly hauled him to his feet and let go with a roundhouse right that caught Bud on the side of the jaw, snapping his head to one side.

"Why you dumb drover you!" Bud roared, his eyes fiery. He landed a haymaker which stunned Curly. Carmody slid out of his saddle and jumped Bud, landing a savage series of kidney punches.

Dillworth dismounted and joined the fray. He kicked Duke in the shin and then brought a heavy right fist down on the top of Duke's head, dropping the man to his knees.

Duke pulled a knife and slashed Dillworth's arm, tearing cloth and flesh and bringing blood.

Gabe plowed into the midst of the brawl. The first thing he did was kick the knife from Duke's hand before it could cut Dillworth again. The second thing he did was bring his knee up to smash against Duke's lower jaw.

As Duke went flying backward, his hat flying off, Gabe turned to find Curly lying unconscious on the ground.

Charley came at Gabe, both of his fists flying, both of them missing Gabe who ducked and weaved and then came in under those flying fists and landed a right uppercut and then a left jab which knocked the wind out of Charley.

Nearby, Bud suddenly let out a roar of triumph as he struck Carmody with the barrel of his drawn gun. Carmody went down and did not stir. Bud turned to confront Dillworth who was heading through the roiling dust toward him. As Dillworth came within range of him, Bud swung his gun again, striking Dillworth on the jaw and drawing blood.

The injured trail boss let out an anguished howl and backed off, cradling his jaw in both hands, then taking his hands away and staring in shock at the bright red blood on them.

Gabe saw the blow coming before he felt it, but he was too late to stop it. Charley landed a left uppercut on the side jaw, and the blow sent little white lights flashing furiously in front of Gabe's dazed eyes.

Through that cluster of flashing lights, he managed to make out another figure moving toward him. It took him only seconds to recognize Duke. He ducked as Duke swung at him, and Duke's fist flew over his head.

He butted Duke with his head, losing his hat in the process, swung around, straightened up, and slammed a savage right fist into Charley's jutting jaw.

Duke staggered backward. Charley drew his gun.

Gabe scooped up dirt and threw it in Charley's face. Then he reached out and seized the barrel of Charley's gun. He got his hand around the cylinder, preventing Charley from firing. Jerking the gun out of his attacker's hand, he fired a shot into the air.

"Fight's over," he announced, his chest heaving. "You three stampeders—get on your mounts and ride on out of here."

In response to his order, a snarling Bud went for his gun. Duke did the same.

Gabe fired two quick shots from Charley's gun. The first knocked the gun Bud had drawn out of his hand. The second shot shattered Duke's hand.

Duke screamed, a series of rising and falling ululations, as he gripped his wounded hand with his good one.

"Am I going to have to tell you again that it's time you three were moving on?" Gabe asked in a deceptively calm tone. "Are you boys slow learners, is that the problem? If it is, I'm a patient man and one who's willing to keep on trying to teach you the lesson it's high time you all learned."

As Gabe brandished Charley's gun and drew his .44 caliber Colt as a backup weapon, Bud, cursing and glaring at Gabe, gestured to his two companions and then climbed aboard his horse.

Charley and Duke did the same.

"Adios," Gabe said, his fingers on the triggers of the two guns in his hands.

The three men rode toward the hummocks.

"Not that way," Gabe ordered. "Head west across the plain. I don't want to lose sight of you behind those hummocks. It's the snakes you can't see that can do you the most harm."

Grumbling and cursing, the three men turned their mounts and headed west, riding away across the open prairie.

CHAPTER TWO

Gabe holstered his Colt revolver. He thrust Charley's gun into his waistband and went over to where his hat lay on the ground. He picked it up and slapped it against his thigh to rid it of dust. Then, clapping it back on his head, he headed for the spot where Dillworth was standing.

On the way, he picked up Duke's knife which lay abandoned on the ground. "You look a little the worse for wear," he commented, giving the trail boss an appraising glance.

"The cut on my arm's not worth fretting about," Dillworth remarked. "I'll get our cook to douse it with alcohol and wrap a piece of muslin around it. As for my jaw though—it feels like half my teeth are ready to fall out."

Gabe glanced at Carmody who was getting to his feet. "You okay?" he inquired.

Carmody gave a noncommittal grunt and helped a dazed Curly to rise from where he was sitting on the ground.

"I've got a gun and a knife that don't belong to me," Gabe said. He offered them both to Dillworth who, without a word, took them from him.

"It's time we moved out after the herd," the trail boss said. "Curly, you and I'll head east. Carmody can scout

south and west of here. Gabe, you ride north and see what
you can find."

"I'll have to get me a mount from the remuda since my
horse was turned into mincemeat by those beeves when
they up and ran like the did," Curly said. "I'll also have
to borrow a saddle, blanket, and bridle from the wrangler
since my gear got trampled to bits when those longhorns
went haywire."

"We'll bring any beeves we find back here, will we?"
Gabe asked.

Dillworth answered his question with a curt nod.

"You've given them a road brand?"

"That's right. A double diamond on the hip."

"Be seeing you boys." With that, Gabe went to his horse,
swung into the saddle, and rode out. He saw no cattle on
the tableland ahead of him which meant that if any of the
longhorns had headed due north they were miles away by
now. He urged his horse into a fast trot and then, when he
still saw no sign of cattle after having covered a good two
miles, into a gallop.

Above him, clouds scudded across the sky. At times,
their dark bulk hid the sun, but then they moved on, the
wind herding them southwest. No trees grew on the prairie
Gabe was crossing so that the wind, which was rising, tore
across the land unimpeded and with full force since there
was nothing to stop it—no hills and no trees. As it worried
his hat, Gabe pulled it down on his forehead so that he
would not lose it in a sudden stiff gust.

He had covered, he estimated, another two miles before
he caught sight of some cattle ahead and to the west of
his position. He turned his horse and headed for them,
hoping they were some of the ones he had been seeking.
He thought the odds were in his favor since there was no
sign of habitation anywhere in the immediate vicinity or
behind him. No soddy, no cultivated fields, no fence.

When he reached the cattle, he was relieved to see the
double diamond burned on the hide covering their hips.
The brands were fresh, the hair around them still singed.
He started to circle the bunch which contained thirty-two

head, intending to turn it and drive it back the way he had
just come. When he reached the far side of the small herd,
he rode toward them.

The cattle scattered in front of him, some of them bawling
in what might have been annoyance or, perhaps, fear. He
rode to the left to bunch them up and then around the rear
of the herd and to the right to accomplish the same purpose
on that side. By continuing his efforts—riding to the left
and then to the right—he managed to keep the drift in a
fairly narrow line.

The clouds in the sky had thickened and grown black.
Rain's coming, he thought, as he *ki-yied* the cattle at the
top of his voice and they continued to drift. When one of
them suddenly made a run for it, Gabe spurred his buckskin
and went after the animal. He was gaining on it when it
suddenly swerved and, as if it knew exactly what it was
doing, tore headlong into a bramble thicket.

Gabe turned his mount in time to avoid the thicket and
the damage it could do to any horse unfortunate enough to
find itself in the middle of the thicket's barbed branches. But
the longhorn didn't seem to mind the brambles. It plowed
on as if it were in the midst of a stand of sweet clover.

Gabe was waiting for it when it finally emerged from the
thicket. The longhorn skidded to a halt and stood there a
moment, its horns swinging from side to side. Then it ran
to the left. Gabe went after it, easing his horse closer to it as
he caught up with it, forcing it to turn and start back toward
the rest of the cows which Gabe could see plodding south
in the distance. It took him several more minutes to get the
longhorn back to the drift. When he finally succeeded in
doing so, the steer readily joined its companions and moved
on with no further display of independence.

Now that he had the animals in line and moving in the
direction he wanted them to go, Gabe was able to travel
almost at a walk. He no longer had to ride from side to
side of the herd. His mere presence now seemed sufficient
to keep them in line.

He and the longhorns had covered about a mile when
the first few drops of rain fell. Gabe looked up at the sky

which was now black. Evening seemed to have settled on the land, judging by the quality of the light, although it was only mid-afternoon. He tightened his grip on his reins and slowed the buckskin. As the herd moved on past him, he took up a position directly behind them and began to move them forward at a faster pace. He hoped he could get back to the temporary cow camp before the full force of what looked to him to be a bad storm hit.

But it was not to be. Thunder rumbled in the distance. The rain began to fall faster. The bawling of the cattle grew louder. The clacking of their horns against one another was an eerie accompaniment to the thunder that was growing louder by the minute. What Gabe had been dreading came a moment later.

The first flash of lightning lit the sky like a thousand lamps turned on all at once. The roiling black thunderheads could be seen in its pale light as clearly as if there were no storm and no sheets of rain pelting Gabe and the cattle in his charge.

He rode up to the head of the herd, picking up his coiled lariat that hung from his saddle horn as he went. When the lead steer showed signs of bolting as jagged lightning flashed again in the sky, he struck the animal across the face with the rope. The steer lowered its head, bawled, and plodded on across the ground that was fast becoming muddy as the rainfall intensified. He continued keeping a wary eye on the steers that walked, blinking their great eyes in the rain, ready and willing to act to prevent a repeat of the earlier stampede, albeit on a smaller scale.

His presence seemed to calm or perhaps intimidate the longhorns; he wasn't sure which. In any event, no stampede started, even though thunder continued to roar in the sky and the lightning repeatedly made its awesome electrical display overhead.

Gabe rode on, his clothes becoming soaked, his eyes on the cattle. The rain made wet mats of the longhorns' hides and dripped from their horns. They were silent now; none of them made a sound.

The lead steer suddenly halted.

Gabe raised his rope, prepared to strike.

Then he saw what had halted the steer. Two jackrabbits were bounding across the trail up ahead. Funny, he thought. Game goes to ground when it rains. So what are those two doing running around out here like it was a fine spring day? He got his answer when the first hailstones struck him.

That's what moved them out of their cover, he realized, as more hailstones began to fall. They came from the west, and that's the way the storm's moving, so the hailstones hit them first before they started falling here.

The sound of the many missiles striking the horns of the cattle was crackling music, a raucous accompaniment to the thunder. A hailstone as large as a robin's egg struck Gabe on the shoulder. That'll leave its mark, he thought. That one hurt. So did the next one that landed on his wrist. That one was bigger than a robin's egg, and it didn't just hit his wrist; it smashed into it, almost fracturing bone when it did so.

Gabe heard an odd sound that was not part of the storm. It took him a minute to realize that the sound had been made by one of the pair of rabbits that had just crossed his trail. The rabbit lay sprawled on the ground off to his right, its legs twitching. Then, as the cattle and Gabe moved past it, it stopped moving.

The hail, Gabe thought. A hailstone cracked the critter's skull. He'd seen it happen before. Hailstones sometimes had the size and strength to kill small game such as rabbits and roadrunners. The missiles continued to strike him and the cattle. One took a piece of skin off the back of his left hand. Another ripped a hole in his right shirt sleeve and pierced the skin of his bicep.

Got to get out of this mess, he told himself. If I don't, I may get skinned by these hailstones. The damned things are getting bigger by the minute. But there was no cover anywhere. No trees. No cave in the side of a hill—no hills, in fact. He drew rein and dismounted. He put on his slicker and then began to whistle and then to sing as he unbuckled his cinch strap.

"I'm up in the morning before daylight.
And before I sleep the moon shines bright.
No chaps and no slicker, and it's pouring down rain,
And I swear, by God, that I'll never night herd again."

The words to the song, *The Old Chisholm Trail*, seemed
to soothe the cattle despite the rain, thunder, lightning, and
hailstones. They began to mill and as they did so, they
circled Gabe and his buckskin. He stripped the saddle from
his horse and got himself ready to step nimbly out of the
way of any longhorn that came too close to him.

"Oh, it's bacon and beans most every day—
I'd as soon be eating prairie hay."

He hunkered down on the ground next to the buckskin
and held his saddle over his head to protect himself from
the onslaught of the still-falling hailstones. They struck the
leather with a steady, thudding tattoo as Gabe continued
crooning one of the traditional lullabies countless cowboys
before him had sung to quiet jittery cows in just situations
as the one he was now facing.

"I went to the boss to draw my roll,
He had it figured out I was nine dollars in the hole.
I'll sell my horse and I'll sell my saddle;
You can go to hell with your longhorn cattle."

The cattle, still slowly milling around Gabe and his buckskin, shook their heads in a futile attempt to ward off the
large hailstones that were still falling. Their horns collided
as they did so, making a loud clatter that almost drowned
out the sound of the thunder that had begun to fade as the
storm moved on.

Gabe continued singing, trying to ignore the pain the
hailstones brought to his exposed fingers as they continued
to hold his saddle over his head. He also tried to ignore the
weariness in his arms that came from holding up the saddle

to protect himself from the hailstones' icy onslaught. He had stopped singing and taken to whistling when the rain slowed and then finally stopped.

The longhorns began to bawl as if to welcome the sight of the sun that appeared briefly in a break in the clouds and then promptly disappeared again.

Gabe rose and placed his saddle on the ground. Keeping one eye on the cattle and the other on what he was doing, he wrung out his saddle blanket and then put it, reluctantly, back on his buckskin.

"You'll have to put up with it wet till we get back to the cow camp," he told the horse as he placed his saddle on the animal and secured it. "It's not too far to travel so you'll survive. I promise you I'll take good care of you once we get to where we're going."

Gabe swung into the saddle and moved the steers out, herding them into a narrow drift and heading them south. The remainder of the journey was uneventful except for the fact that the longhorns swung sharply to the left at one point. Gabe saw what it was that had disturbed them—a dead prairie dog that had evidently been caught out of its burrow when the storm hit. Its body had lost most of its fur which had been stripped away by the merciless pelting of the hailstones that had killed it.

When he got to the cow camp, he was glad to see that the cook had a fire going and was busy with his pots and pans and a Dutch oven. The smell of food cooking made Gabe's mouth salivate. He moved the cattle he had rounded up over to where scores of others were grazing on what would become their bed ground when night came. Then, Gabe led his buckskin inside the rope corral the wrangler had strung on the leeward side of the camp so that the dust the horses raised and the odor of their droppings would not reach the men in the camp.

He stripped his gear from the buckskin and proceeded to wipe it down, using handfuls of grass to accomplish the task. The horse's hide rippled with sensuous pleasure under his hands, and when he had finished what he was doing the animal nickered as if to thank its master for his services.

Gabe was hanging his saddle blanket up to dry on a low limb of a post oak tree when Dave Carmody appeared.

"How many did you bring in?" Carmody asked gruffly.

Gabe told him. "Has everybody come back that went off to hunt cows?"

"All but Curly. He's still on the scout, but Mr. Dillworth came on back with close to a hundred head him and Curly rounded up."

"How many were killed in the stampede?"

"Thirty-one that we know of. Maybe more. We won't know for sure till Curly gets back. The rest of them'll take a while to get back the weight they ran off of themselves. Mr. Dillworth says we can stop for a spell once we cross Red River."

"Stop? You mean in Chickasaw Nation?"

"What's the matter, Conrad? You scared of Injuns?"

Gabe ignored the jibe. "Spending time on Chickasaw land could prove costly from what I hear."

"What do you mean? What have you heard?"

"The Chickasaws have taken, I'm told, to charging for the use of their land for grazing. I hear they're requiring drovers to purchase permits for the right to move herds through their land."

"Mr. Dillworth didn't say nothing about permits or any such thing to me. I reckon he knows what he's doing. He's not likely to let no Injuns tell him what he can or can't do."

"Well, we'll see about that, won't we?" Gabe said as he ducked under the rope and left the corral.

He was on his way to the chuck wagon when Curly appeared in the distance. The man was standing up in his stirrups and *ki-yieing* the cattle he had located as he drove them toward the main body of the herd on the far side of the camp.

"I brought in fifty-three more head, Mr. Dillworth!" Curly crowed as he rode into camp and dismounted. "Two head ran off a ledge into a draw and busted their legs. I had to put them out of their misery."

"Good work, Curly," Dillworth said from where he stood next to the chuck wagon, cradling a tin cup filled with coffee in his gnarled hands.

"Hey, Cook," Curly yelled. "Is supper ready? I'm starving. My gut thinks my throat's been cut."

The cook responded with a clanging of pots and pans and a muttered curse.

Curly laughed and led his horse over to the corral.

He came running back when the cook called out, "Come and get it or do without!"

Gabe availed himself of a tin plate, cup, and a knife and fork and then joined the other drovers in the chow line. When he got to the cook, the man filled his plate with a beefless stew containing an odd mixture of onions, potatoes, and a few pinto beans. He helped himself to a pair of biscuits, poured himself a cup of coffee, and went over to where Curly was seated cross-legged on the ground, hungrily devouring the food on his plate.

"Bland," Gabe commented after hunkering down and spooning some of the stew into his mouth.

"We ran out of salt two days ago," Curly said through a mouthful of food. "What I do is lick the sweat from my horse to get some salt. You ever hear of that trick?"

"I've not only heard of it, I've tried it a time or two myself when I was next door to desperate."

"We also ran out of beef, and Mr. Dillworth'll never let us kill one of our beeves for meat now, not with the losses we suffered in the stampede, he won't."

"A man can live without beef."

"I reckon so, but it's not the best kind of living, is it?" Without waiting for an answer from Gabe, Curly continued, "Trail driving—it's a hard life lived without a lot of things that make life nice and easy. Like a feather bed. Like a decent woman." Curly grinned at Gabe and added, "Or the two of them put together—the woman and a soft feather bed. If you take my meaning."

"I take it and I have to agree with you."

"I don't know why I do it. I don't know why anybody does it, I truly don't."

"You're talking about cowboying?"

Curly nodded. "Ever since I was hock high to a short horse, I've wanted to live the life of a cowboy. I used to think it was the only life for a real man. I never could see myself marching behind a plow for a living. Or living in some town full of politeness and too many laws.

"No, it was always the cowboy kind of life I hankered hard after. Now that I got it, I think maybe I ought to have had my head examined." Curly chuckled and ate the last of his food.

"The grass always does look greener on the far side of the fence," Gabe observed and then drank some of his coffee.

"It gets tiresome looking at the world from between a horse's ears."

"You could settle down somewhere, Curly. Find yourself a nice girl. Buy yourself a feather bed." It was Gabe's turn to grin.

"Maybe someday," Curly said with a soft sigh. "Yeah, maybe." He was silent for a long moment. Then, "That's kind of the story of my life. Those two words sum it up, sure enough."

"What two words?"

"Maybe someday. It's a fitting motto for somebody like me who keeps chasing will-o'-the-wisps from can-see to can't-see."

"Carmody tells me we'll be letting the herd take its ease once we cross the Red and move into Chickasaw Nation."

"So I hear. Mr. Dillworth wants to put some bulk back on our beeves. Even if we get to do that, they could stampede again and run it all off. Mr. Dillworth won't get top dollar for these cattle once he gets them to Dodge if that keeps up. Hell, longhorns are stringy enough without they run themselves halfway round the world for no purpose that makes any kind of sense to man nor beast."

"Speaking of crossing the Red, we may have our hands full doing that once we get there."

"You mean because of all the rain we've been having the past week?"

Gabe nodded. "I've seen Red River when it's running high. It can be treacherous."

"This old world of ours, it sure is a prickly kind of place, ain't it though? What with cattle stampedes and flooded rivers and the Lord alone knows what else, including twisters that seem to pop up every day and twice on Sunday up in Indian Territory where we, fools that we be, are headed."

Gabe could do nothing but agree with Curly's wry comment.

"Conrad!"

He turned to find Carmody beckoning to him. He rose, handed his plate, cup, and eating irons to the wrangler who was collecting them, and headed for Carmody who was worrying his teeth with a wooden toothpick.

"You'll take first watch," Carmody announced when Gabe reached him. "Your horse a good night horse? If he's not, the wrangler can give you Old Blue who can see in the dark and tell time by the stars."

"My mount's as good in the dark as he is in the day."

"Go get him then and be on your way."

Gabe did as he was told, glad to find that his saddle blanket had dried in the light breeze that was blowing across the prairie. He got his buckskin ready to ride and then swung into the saddle. Turning the horse, he headed away from the cow camp toward the spot where the cattle were moving like great bulk shadows in the deepening dusk.

Some of them were lowing; one or two had already slumped down on the ground for the night. When he reached the herd, he began to bed them down for the night by circling them in an ever-diminishing spiral path. It took him half an hour to accomplish his purpose, a half hour during which the last of the stars blazed to bright life in a sky that was empty of clouds.

In the distance he could hear the faint strains of the cow camp guard singing—off-key—the interminable verses of *Dinah Had a Wooden Leg*. As the night grew older, *Dinah* gave way to a melancholy version of *The Unfortunate Pup*.

The light of the campfire grew steadily weaker as the minutes passed until finally it became only a small orange

eye blinking in the dark. The cattle had become quiet now,
he noted, as his buckskin moved surefootedly through the
darkness. No shadow spooked the horse. No sound startled
it. The hoot of an owl brought only a faint answering nicker
from the horse. The buckskin picked its way easily and
safely across the dark gullied land as it continued carrying
its rider in a circle around the silent herd.

Gabe drew rein some time later and sat his saddle, his
hands wrapped around his saddle horn as he surveyed the
longhorns sleeping in the quiet night. Big money on the
hoof, he thought. He wondered at the mysterious ways of
the world. Why were these not his cattle on their way to
market at the railhead in Dodge? By what quirk of fate was
he here guarding other men's cows and those other men
were somewhere else, maybe dining in a richly appointed
restaurant with women of brilliant beauty whose laughter
was a fine rich music.

He smiled to himself in the darkness. Let the men, the
owners of these sleeping longhorns, enjoy their lives and
their riches. He had riches of his own on which no man,
least of all himself, could put a price. He had the entire
West—indeed, the world if he wanted it—in which to roam
under the invisible banner he bore always with him, the
name of which was Freedom. A priceless commodity. It
was the gateway to wonder. It was the highway to marvels,
if not miracles. If it was sometimes a dangerous highway,
one fraught with peril, then let it be so. Peril was the spice
that made freedom piquant. It was the tangy ingredient in
the complex mixture that was a man's life without which
some men, men like himself, would find life hardly worth
living.

He had his own ways to be practiced in his own good
time with no man to tell him what he must do or when and
how he must do it. At times he took orders, as he did now
on this trail drive he had willingly joined, only because he
wanted to. At other times, he took orders from no man.

If what he found at the end of a trail displeased him
in any way, he could saddle up and follow another trail,
perhaps one less traveled, perhaps one men warned was

dangerous, in search of whatever he wanted at the time.
When he found it, he would be content—for a time. Then,
when the restlessness arose again within him, he had the
freedom to move on, following the beckoning figure of
Fate whose features were always hidden and whose nature
no man knew.

What he did not have was almost as valuable to him as
what he did have. He had no ties to bind him to any town
or any particular place. He had no debts of any kind he had
not paid. He had no master.

The owl he had heard earlier suddenly swooped down
out of a sycamore, a dark shadow against the full moon
for a moment, then rose again, a field mouse clutched in
its talons, and disappeared in the darkness.

That's the way of things, Gabe found himself thinking.
For man or beast there's no guarantee he'll be gifted with
the next minute let alone the next day or month or year. That
mouse the owl caught no doubt thought he was going to be
here forever. It certainly never thought it would wind up in
the belly of some hunting hoot owl. The critter should have
kept a wary eye open. But maybe it did and still it turned
into fodder for a critter keener than itself. There's no one,
he thought, to mourn the mouse's passing, no one even to
note it other than himself. Same thing happens to a man—
to some men at least. Men like himself who rode the trails
for their allotted days and then were seen no more. Was
there ever anyone left somewhere—a mother, a friend—to
wonder at such men's vanishings?

He looked up at the polestar. Close to ten o'clock. He
glanced over his shoulder toward the camp. The fire had
burned down low now and was only a faint shimmer of
light in the night's enveloping blackness that the moon and
stars could not dispel. There was movement there. He could
just barely make out a dim figure rising up from the ground
like an apparition. The man was hopping from one foot to
the other as he pulled on his pants. When the man was
dressed, he walked to the rope corral, cut loose a horse,
and mounted it. Gabe was still watching as the man rode
through the darkness toward him.

"Any trouble?" he asked when he had joined Gabe.

"None. The beeves are sleeping like babies, most of them."

"Good thing after that stampede we had. My name's Driscoll. Tim Driscoll. Didn't have a chance to make your acquaintance before now, Conrad. I think maybe Mr. Dillworth started that stampede just to make sure I'd earn my forty dollars and found on this trip we're making."

"You don't really think—"

"Just joshing."

Driscoll eyed the cattle scattered on the bed ground. "I hope Curly doesn't sleep in like he's prone to do. I hope he shows up to relieve me on time. This mount of mine, he's got some crazy ideas about time, he has. Never knew a horse like him and never want to know another one like him. Big Jack here, he's got a head full of notions that I for one can't fathom. Take time, like I mentioned. Big Jack won't no way stand a night watch of more than two hours. If my relief—Curly in this instance—doesn't show up by midnight what I'll have to do is I'll have to ride Big Jack back to camp, dismount, wake up Curly, and then ride back here to wait for Curly to get dressed and take over from me. All that to make Big Jack think he's starting a brand-new two-hour watch. It's the only way to fool him. Otherwise, he'll start champing at the bit the minute the polestar is northeast of the Big Dipper and it's turned two o'clock."

"Be seeing you, Driscoll," Gabe said and rode back to the camp. After returning his buckskin to the corral, he found himself a place close to the fire to bed down. He pulled off his boots, took off his hat, and unbuckled his gun belt. After spreading his tarp and placing his blanket on it, he positioned his saddle to serve as a pillow.

He lay down with his revolver close at hand, shifting position to get comfortable, and closed his eyes.

A rustling sound caused him to open them. He saw a sleeper rise and take a seat on a log by the fire. He watched the man build and light a quirly and sit there smoking in his long johns. Another man stirred in his sleep and whispered a name: "Lucy." Other men tightly clutched the pillows they had made by bundling their pants and shirts together. Some of them snored. Others slept soundlessly, never moving a muscle.

Gabe closed his eyes again, leaving the night to the insomniac and his smoke. He felt sleep stealing up on him and let it come. It had been a long day. A hard day. He drifted off into a sound sleep and eventually into a dream of his days among the Oglala Sioux.

He was a boy again playing shinny in the camp of the People. It was a bright spring day, and he was chosen to play for the north team against the south team. The bets of jewelry, clothing, and weapons had been made and matched and safely stored in the meeting lodge.

He stripped off his robe and leggings, unbraided his hair, and painted his face as was the custom in the game. He waited with the members of his and the opposing team for the referee—a man named Goes On Long Journeys— to throw the small leather ball up into the air.

When Goes On Long Journeys did so, Gabe raced toward it, the bent ash shinny stick clutched tightly in his hands. When he got to where it lay on the ground, he struck it with his shinny stick. It almost hit the south tipi to score a goal but missed it by about two feet.

The spectators on the sidelines cheered his effort and he tried again to score, but a player on the south team knocked him off his feet and scored a goal by striking the leather ball so hard it almost tore through the hide wall of the north tipi.

Then the north team, with Gabe running interference, scored a goal. Both teams kept at it with a kind of rigidly controlled fury then since the game would be won by the team that scored two out of a total of three goals.

"Long Rider, go!" a young girl called from the sideline as the play moved far afield. "Score, Long Rider!"

He knew who it was. Her name was She Runs, and he had many times seen her smile his way.

The crowd cheered. He swung his shinny stick.

"Come and get it!"

Gabe awoke to find the sun climbing above the horizon and the cook ready to serve breakfast. He sat up and threw off his blanket. He shook out his boots to make sure they contained no insect life and then pulled them on. He rose, clapped his hat on his head, and strapped on his gunbelt. Adjusting it so that it hung high on his hip, he went to the water barrel that was strapped to the chuck wagon, turned the spigot, and splashed water on his face. Then, taking a plate and utensils from the chuck wagon box, he got in the line that was composed of yawning drovers. When the cook plopped a boiled mixture of rice and raisins on the plate of the man in front of Gabe, the cowboy looked at the cook and muttered, "That's it?"

"That's it," the cook blustered. "I told Mr. Dillworth we're low on supplies. Fact of the matter is, that's the last of the raisins. The dried apples ran out two days back. What's more, we've not got enough flour to last till we get to Red River where we can stock up on provisions. I'm not even so sure I can stretch the beans till then neither. Move on, mister."

The man did so, grumbling under his breath, and Gabe received his share of the rice and raisin mixture which, he found after tasting it, wasn't half bad.

By the time he had finished his meal, the drovers were getting ready to move out. They were cutting out of the remuda their first horse of the day and tossing their tarpaulin-wrapped quilts into the chuck wagon. Gabe tied his bedroll behind the cantle of his saddle once he had his buckskin ready to ride. He swung into the saddle to the dissonant tune of clanging Dutch ovens as the cook stowed his equipment and the chuck box aboard his wagon preparatory to moving out. Behind Gabe, the wrangler was taking down his rope corral.

"Throw them on the trail, boys!" Dillworth called out from where he was sitting his saddle and watching the drovers as they circled the cattle which were slowly getting to their feet.

Gabe, together with the other drovers, closed in on the broad drift of animals and began to squeeze them into a ragged line of march. The man on his left called out, "Ho cattle, ho ho ho *ho!*" Two of the drovers took upon themselves the task of riding out to chase back strays that wandered away.

"Morning, Gabe," Curly said as he rode up beside Gabe.

"Good morning."

"Damn calves," Curly muttered. "They sure do make a drive go poorly. If I had my way, I'd sign on drives that only had steers, no cows and no calves. Listen to 'em. The cows sound like a pipe organ the way they're groaning and moaning while they search for their young 'uns."

Dillworth rode up beside the pair. "Move them along at a fast clip. There's a heavy dew on the grass this morning so don't let them graze. If we don't set them to stepping sprightly the dew'll soften their hooves."

"Yes, sir, Mr. Dillworth," Curly responded and moved his mount closer to the drift. He gave a steer a kick with one booted foot to send it trotting forward at a brisk pace.

Gabe rode at a steady pace as he helped to keep the drift in line, leaving the strays to other drovers. He was aware of the sounds of the cattle's ankle joints cracking as they plodded along, of their hooves thudding on the hard ground, of their long horns occasionally clattering together. He became aware of a thin plume of smoke rising off to the east beyond a barely visible furrow fence.

Hours later, Dillworth, who was in front of the herd, began to ride in a circle. Then he stopped broadside to the herd, his horse's head pointing in the direction he wanted his men to drive the cattle where the animals would be left to graze while the trail hands made their nooning.

CHAPTER THREE

The drovers ate in shifts so that two of them could at all times ride an easy watch—loose herd—over the cattle.

"We've covered about five miles, I'd estimate," Dillworth told his men as he sipped a cup of coffee while standing beside the chuck wagon. "We'll let these beeves graze a bit when we move them out. We'll still probably cover another two or three miles this afternoon."

"How long before we reach Red River?" one of the drovers asked the trail boss.

"We'll get there in another two, three days if the weather holds and nothing spooks the cattle into making another run."

"I can't wait till we get to Red River," the same man said. "At last—a little civilized company instead of a bunch of smelly cussing cowboys to put up with."

He was immediately jumped on verbally by his companions who told him nobody civilized would want to get within a country mile of him and that he wouldn't know civilization from a two-story chicken coop.

Gabe was on his way to turn his buckskin over to the wrangler in exchange for a fresh horse when he spotted a cow that seemed to be in distress. He walked over to her, leading his horse. Closer inspection of the animal revealed that she was just going into labor. But then, to his surprise, the cow lay down on the ground instead of remaining on her feet, her eyes wide with alarm as she strained and muscles rippled beneath her hide.

"What's holding things up?" Carmody asked as he appeared at Gabe's side. "Usually these pregnant critters drop their calves as easy as eating apple pie."

"She's having a hard time of it," Gabe observed. "Maybe this is her first." He watched as the cow's sides heaved and her breathing began to come in ragged little bursts.

Gabe continued watching while Carmody cursed the delay the pregnant cow was causing. The animal pushed and strained as hard as she could without any sign of her calf appearing. Mucus dripped from her nostrils as her breath whistled in and out. She blinked repeatedly, and her tail rose and fell, rose and fell.

Carmody drew his gun, prepared to shoot the laboring animal.

Gabe put out a hand and stopped him from doing so. "Mr. Dillworth won't be overjoyed to lose another head of beef, Carmody, so why don't you put that gun away while I see what I can do for this poor critter."

"Suit yourself. But it strikes me that it would make more sense to kill that cow or leave her behind than to lose time on the trail again. If she does manage to deliver, her calf will only slow us up."

"You may be right but, like I said, give me a chance to see what, if anything, I can do for her."

Gabe got down on one knee beside the cow that was already close to exhaustion and placed a hand on her heaving flank. He noted her swollen and rigid udder as he gently stroked her. He saw the droplets of milk leaking from her teats. As he bent down for a closer look, the calf's hind hooves with the pads up appeared. Almost immediately, they jerked back up inside the cow.

"Breech birth," Carmody declared, his gun still in his hand.

"Uh-huh. She's presenting her calf backward—hind feet first instead of with the calf's head nestled nice and snug between its two front feet. The calf's all twisted up inside her—its hind hoof pads were facing up just now when they popped out for a minute. This lady needs some help and she needs it real bad. Maybe I can give it to her."

Gabe stopped stroking the cow's flank and rose. He took his lariat from his saddle horn and then got down on both knees beside the cow that was eyeing him nervously. He began speaking to her in a soft voice. He told her he knew she had a problem but between the two of them he reckoned they had a fair to fine chance of solving it. He told her he understood why she had given up and lain down instead of standing up to drop her calf nice and easy.

Gabe cut two lengths of rope from his lariat and waited, still encouraging the cow in soft tones. The instant the calf's two hind hooves reappeared, he tied the lengths of rope to them. Then, rising, he braced himself and began to pull on the ropes.

"Keep trying, old girl," he said between gritted teeth. "Don't give up the good fight now."

The cow raised her weary head and stared at him with her luminous brown eyes before lowering her head again and letting it rest on the ground. Gabe spoke to her, almost pleaded with her, when he saw that she had given up straining to deliver her calf. His words seemed to encourage her. When she began to strain again, her large body quivering, he pulled hard on the ropes and another two inches of the calf's hind legs appeared.

He continued his strenuous efforts as the cow continued trying desperately to deliver her offspring. "It's not going to work," he said to Carmody several minutes later.

"Step aside then. I'll shoot her."

"No. I'm going to try to turn the calf inside her." He dropped the two ropes and stood up. Stripping off his shirt, he went back to the chuck wagon where he got some lye soap from the cook. At the water barrel, he thoroughly washed his right arm and then went back to where Carmody was watching him with a perplexed expression on his weathered face.

Gabe knelt beside the cow and waited a moment until

she stopped straining. Then, leaning down close to her, he began to croon a wordless tune he hoped would help her relax. When he was reasonably sure she was not about to begin straining again, he placed his hand beside the calf's protruding hind legs and eased his hand into the mother. She lowed and began to tremble. He continued his crooning as his wrist and then his forearm disappeared inside the cow.

He felt along the length of the calf's hind legs and then got a firm grip on both of them. Slowly he began to turn the unborn calf within the uterine walls. The calf resisted, causing him to curse under his breath. When the cow lowed again and stirred nervously, Gabe knelt on her hind legs to keep her from kicking him.

No longer crooning now but grunting with the effort he was making, he let go of the calf's hind legs and thrust his arm farther up inside the laboring cow. He got a grip on the calf's stretched-out body and, bending over at a sharp angle, at last managed to turn it.

Relief flooded him as the cow immediately began to strain again and he felt the calf pushing against his arm, which he promptly withdrew. The cow's body gave a sudden convulsive movement and then, shuddering violently, she delivered her offspring.

Gabe quickly removed the ropes from the newborn's hind legs. Then, getting to his feet, he picked up the dripping newborn which was littered with pieces of torn placenta. He stood up, and holding the blinking animal in his arms, its legs dangling, he turned to Carmody with a big grin on his face.

"Well, you did it," Carmody declared with grudging admiration as he holstered his gun.

Gabe, still grinning, watched the cow lumber to her feet and stand there tottering unsteadily for several seconds. Then he put the calf down on its feet beside its mother and laughed as its legs gave way under it and the calf fell down. He bent down and helped it rise.

He nudged the calf toward its mother who promptly began to lick it and then to eat the tattered placenta. This would help her make lots of milk for her calf. Gabe bent down and thrust an index finger into the calf's mouth. Then, as the animal instinctively began to suck on his finger, he lifted it, placed it next to its mother and replaced his finger in its mouth with one of the cow's teats. He stepped back and stood watching with satisfaction as the wobbly newborn nursed.

"Carmody!"

Carmody turned to find Dillworth watching him as the other drovers began to move the herd out. "Get to work! You too, Conrad."

As Gabe gave him a nod in acknowledgment of his order, Dillworth rode up to him and Carmody.

"What's this? You two turning into midwives?"

"Conrad delivered that calf," Carmody said as if to place the blame squarely where it belonged.

"I figured you wouldn't want to lose the cow," Gabe told the trail boss by way of explanation. "She was having a breech birth. I stepped in and lent her a hand."

"I'm obliged to you for saving the cow," Dillworth said. "As for the calf—shoot it, Carmody."

Carmody gave Gabe an I-told-you-so look and drew his gun.

"Hold on, Carmody," Gabe said. "Mr. Dillworth, if you'll give me an hour or so, I think I might be able to work something out so you won't have to shoot that newborn. A way that'll turn it into an asset for you."

"We've wasted enough time on this drive already," Dillworth shot back. "I don't want to waste any more time, and that calf will play havoc with the herd, slow it down—"

"Mr. Dillworth, you gave the order to let the herd graze on the trail this afternoon. Why not let it graze now? Here? Then, when I get back—"

"Where are you going?" Dillworth asked.

"When I get back," Gabe continued, ignoring the question, "if I've failed to work out what I have in mind to your benefit, you can go ahead and shoot the calf, and we can make up the lost time this afternoon with no grazing permitted on the trail. That amounts to six of one and half a dozen of the other, I'd say."

Dillworth and Carmody exchanged glances, and then Dillworth said, "One hour. If you're not back by then, Carmody shoots the calf and we move on without you."

Gabe sprinted over to the chuck wagon, hurriedly washed his bloody arm, put his shirt back on, and then headed for the remuda.

Minutes later, aboard a high-stepping dapple he had gotten from the wrangler, he was riding back the way they had come that morning.

When Gabe returned less than an hour later, he was riding beside a wagon driven by a pipe-smoking, middle-aged man.

As Dillworth walked up to the wagon, Gabe dismounted and said, "This here's Mr. Soames. Soames, this is our trail boss I told you about. Meet Mr. Dillworth."

The two men shook hands, and then Dillworth shot Gabe a quizzical glance.

"Mr. Soames has come to do some bartering with you," Gabe announced in response to the trail boss' look.

"Bartering? What are you talking about, Conrad?"

"He says you got a calf you're willing to part with," Soames said. "A calf, he says, that'll turn in time into a fine milch cow. That true?"

Dillworth's jaw dropped. He looked from Gabe to Soames and back again.

"Well, is it or ain't it true?" Soames prompted. "I brought goods to barter with, but if you don't want to trade, I'll turn around and head on home."

"No, don't do that," Dillworth said quickly. "It's true I've got a newborn calf I want to get shut of. What's your best offer?"

"I've got flour, salt, sugar, bacon, coffee, beans—what's your pleasure?"

"Wait a minute," Dillworth said. "I'll call the cook. He knows better than I do what we're most in need of."

When the cook had joined them, the bargaining began in

earnest. It started with the cook, backed up by Dillworth, demanding the entire store of provisions Soames had in his wagon bed in return for the calf.

Soames balked. "They're worth calf and cow both," he protested.

"We'll keep the cow," Dillworth interjected.

The cook and Soames went at it then, Soames protesting that the price was too high in goods and the cook insisting that, when Soames figured in the value of all the milk he'd get over the life of the calf-turned-cow and the calves it would have, the wagon load of provisions was cheap.

But Soames remained adamant. "What about the cost of fodder to feed the critter for the rest of its natural life? That counts on the red ink side of the ledger in this here swap. So does the baby bottle I'll have to buy to nurse the critter."

Finally, Dillworth stepped in again, in the interest of saving time, as he put it. Prodded by the trail boss, the cook and Soames came to a settlement. Quantities of flour, beans, sugar, precious salt, coffee, and bacon left the wagon and were stored in the chuck box. The calf was taken from its bawling mother and placed in the wagon bed.

After shaking hands with the cook, Soames drove away, the sound of the bereft cow following him as her baby was taken away from her.

"How the hell did you know Soames was living around here?" Dillworth asked Gabe when the wagon had disappeared from sight.

"Saw smoke back along the trail," Gabe answered.

"You saw smoke, did you? I see. Well, let me ask you this. How did you know the smoke was coming from a house and not, say, from some drifter's campfire?"

"Didn't know for sure," Gabe admitted. "But it was pretty high up in the sky before the wind got to it and blew it away. I figured that must mean it was coming from a chimney, not the ground. If it had been coming from a campfire, the wind would probably have blown it away before I could catch sight of it is the way I figured. Then, too, there was the matter of the furrow fence."

"I didn't see any furrow fence along the trail," Dillworth said.

"I did," Gabe said. "It was kind of hard to spot. It had been plowed a while ago, and the rain had pretty much leveled it, and clover was growing in it. But it was there."

"You must have the eyes of an eagle," Dillworth muttered. "For which I have to say I'm grateful. That calf was of no use to the drive—in fact, it would have been a hindrance, like I said."

"I've heard folk say that one man's trash is another man's treasure. Like in this particular case."

"You said it, Conrad," a smiling Dillworth declared. "Now, let's get a move on. I mean for us to cover five, six miles before dark sets in."

Two and a half days later, in the early evening as dusk was spilling its load of purple shadows across the land, Dillworth left his herd of longhorns outside of town under guard and with Dave Carmody and Gabe by his side strode into the border village of Red River Station.

Already the place was alive with laughter and drunken shouting. Saloons were doing a roaring business. Women with paint on their faces and lust in their eyes loitered on the streets or on the porches of parlor houses sporting lighted red-paned trainman's lanterns over their doors.

Dillworth and Carmody headed for the nearest saloon. When the trail boss realized Gabe was not with him, he turned and called, "Come on, Conrad. Time to wet your whistle."

Gabe didn't want a drink. In fact, he never drank anything stronger than sarsaparilla. But he had learned from experience that to say so almost always led to jeering words or, worse, arguments and, on one ugly occasion he wished he could forget, gunplay. So he waved Dillworth and Carmody on, saying only, "I'd like to take a peek at the town first. Maybe I'll run into you boys later on."

As Dillworth and Carmody went eagerly through the batwings into the saloon, Gabe started down the dirt street that was crowded with wagons and men on horseback. He could smell the river before he could see it. The water had a pungent smell that was not altogether unpleasant. Soon it came into sight. So did the cluster of crudely marked graves on both of its banks which held the remains of cowboys who had died in the river's currents or had been caught in its treacherous quicksand. The wooden crosses and the names and dates painted on them were like silent indictments of the Red River for having claimed the occupants of the graves— for having cut them down in their prime, for stealing from them years and the pleasures waiting within those years.

Gabe stood on the river's bank and looked down at the water below. It flowed west to east and was now almost placid. But it could become, he knew, a raging torrent in a matter of hours due either to sudden heavy rain or similar storms in the distant western mountains where the river had its headwater or a deadly combination of both. The Red might be flowing peacefully along at a depth of a mere six inches or so and then, as a result of storms here or farther west, it could become a raging torrent in less than a day.

Gabe had seen no other herds bedded down outside of town which probably meant that other herds arriving earlier had not paused long in town but had more or less immediately crossed the river, taking advantage of its shallowness which offered a relatively easy ford.

Glancing up and down the river, he noted the tangles of driftwood and torn clothing caught in the upper branches of the cottonwoods that lined both banks of the river. The debris was silent but eloquent testimony to the power of the river and the height to which it could rapidly rise.

He gazed across to the opposite bank—and another world. Over there was the world of Chickasaw Nation. Over there white men did not rule as they did here in Texas. Over there old customs and even older rituals unknown to white men prevailed and sometimes clashed with those of the white world.

A sense of sadness settled on Gabe as he stood there staring into the gathering darkness. For the thousandth time he found himself wondering where he belonged. Here in Texas in a world as white as snow? Or over there in that world that was no more primitive really than the one he was now in? As usual, he found no answer to his question and that fact made the sadness he was feeling especially strong.

The night's deepening darkness seemed to settle on his very soul and seal it with a cold touch that chilled him through and through. He tried to shrug the feeling off. But it would not be totally banished. He carried it with him as he turned and walked away from the river and the unfamiliar world beyond it.

He made his way through the crooked streets of Red River Station with a particular destination in mind. On the way, he speculated that the house for which he was heading might no longer be there. Or if it was still there it might now be inhabited by others than the ones who had lived in it when he was last in this border village.

The last of the sadness he had been feeling left him when he turned a corner—and there it was. Yellow lamplight seeped around the edges of the shades covering its open front windows. Faint music drifted through the partially open windows—the tinkle of a pianoforte. He was smiling as he climbed the steps and used the brass knocker to announce his presence on the porch.

The door was opened a moment later by a fortyish woman with an ample figure. Her blond hair was piled high on her head and held in place by a tortoise shell ornament. There were rings on many of her ten fat fingers and a lace handkerchief tucked provocatively in her ample cleavage. Her face was powdered and her lips rouged.

She peered into the darkness at Gabe through narrowed eyes as the music of the pianoforte drifted out the door into the street. "Come on in, honey, we're open for business."

As she stepped aside, Gabe moved into the lamplight flooding the parlor beyond the door. As the woman closed the door behind him, he turned to her and said, "How've you been Mrs. Morrison?"

She gave him a sharp look that beetled her brow and then exclaimed, "It's you, isn't it?"

"Last time I looked, yep."

She hurried up to him and threw her fleshy arms around him. Her hug squeezed the breath from his lungs. "Gabe Conrad, you are a sight for sore eyes. How long has it been? Six months?"

"More like a year, Mrs. Morrison."

She let him go and stepped back. "Shame on you. Letting a year go by without coming by to see me, your best girl."

"I know I've been remiss, but I've been here and there and yonder, and this is the first time I've been back in Red River Station in all that time. Maybe you can find it in your heart to forgive me if I tell you I've missed you."

Mrs. Morrison hugged him again and then held him out at arm's length and gazed dreamily into his eyes. "If I were twenty years younger—you'd never get out of here alive!"

He joined in her throaty laughter.

"But since I'm not twenty years younger—Gabe, she's still with me."

"Nancy?"

"Who else would I be talking about? I know you have a soft spot in your heart for her and always have since the day you two first met. I'll call her."

When Mrs. Morrison returned, she had with her a young woman whose figure was as slim as the madam's was fulsome. Nancy had the liquid eyes of a doe. Their color matched her dark brown hair which she wore coiled at the nape of her neck in a surprisingly demure fashion considering her chosen profession. She wore no jewelry. Her simple dress was of silk, green and full-skirted.

"Gabe," she said softly. "It's good to see you again. It's been a while."

"Too long a time, honey," he said. He went to where she stood, took her hand, and kissed it.

"Always so gallant," she murmured, her voice sounding both sweet and sensuous to Gabe's ears.

"You two will want to go upstairs," Mrs. Morrison remarked. "You'll want to talk about old times—and so on." She winked at Gabe.

He winked back and then offered his arm to Nancy. He led her out of the room and up the stairs to the second floor.

Once in her bedroom, he closed the door, took her in his arms, and kissed her passionately.

When their kiss ended, Nancy stepped back. Smiling at Gabe, she slid her dress over one shoulder. Then she slid it over her other shoulder. Without taking her eyes from Gabe, she reached behind her and began to unbutton it.

Gabe stood transfixed as he watched her slip out of her dress to reveal the fact that she was wearing nothing at all beneath it. She stood there before him, a vision of loveliness. He went to her and gladly accepted her eager embrace.

"That was wonderful," Nancy whispered, lying next to Gabe. "It feels so good to be so relaxed. So peaceful. As if everything's right with the world."

"Mmmm-hmmm."

"Are you going to be in town for long, Gabe?"

"Uh-uh."

"How long will you be here?"

"I'm with a trail drive heading up to Dodge. The trail boss stocked up on supplies when we got here earlier today. He says we'll head out at first light in the morning."

Nancy propped herself up on one elbow and looked down at Gabe, pouting prettily. "You never stay long when you come to town. You're always on your way somewhere."

"But I always come back, don't I?"

"Next time you do I might not be here, did you ever think of that?"

"I have, but so far I've been lucky. You've been here whenever I showed up."

"Men," Nancy exclaimed with scorn in her voice. "They expect women to sit and wait on their pleasure. It's just not fair!"

"You're wrong about that, honey. You know what they say about all things being fair in love and war."

"When will you be back?"

"I can't answer you that. I don't know when I'll get back here."

"Oh, Gabe!"

"Don't look so sad, Nancy. We'll meet again someday. If not here, somewhere else."

"If that's true—well, the thought's a comfort."

Gabe groaned.

"What's the matter?"

"Listen. Hear that rain starting to hit the window?"

"What about it?"

Gabe reached up and tweaked Nancy's nose. "I hate going out in the rain. I hate sleeping out in the open in it even worse, but that's what I'll have to do I reckon unless—"

"Unless?"

"You let me stay here with you for the night?"

"Mrs. Morrison will expect you to pay for my time."

"I'll pay double if that's what it'll take to spend the night with you. You know that, honey."

"You just want to sleep, is that it?"

"No, that's not it, not by a long shot, it's not. Oh, I do want to sleep part of the night. But not all of it. Maybe not even most of it."

Nancy smiled. "Fine by me," she said.

CHAPTER FOUR

When Gabe arrived at the herd's bed ground early the next morning, most of the men were mounted and getting ready to move the longhorns north to the river.

As he rode into camp, Curly hailed him. "You ready for a swim, Gabe?"

"I'm as ready as I'm going to be."

"I hate water. I can't swim a stroke. I just hope to hell we don't have any trouble. But that rain we had last night, well, the river's bound to be high as a result of it."

Gabe rode over to where the wrangler was looking after his remuda. He bade the boy good morning, transfered his gear from the dapple he was riding to his buckskin, and rode out to join the other drovers.

The clatter of horns and the clacking of the cattle's ankle joints filled the early morning air as the herd began to move sluggishly toward Red River Station. Gabe galloped out after a pair of recalcitrant cows which evidently had notions about heading in a different direction and drove them back into the main drift. Other drovers were doing the same. The sound of "Ho ho ho cattle ho!" rang in the air from more than one throat. Dust rose in the air, and the wind sent it swirling to the west. As they tended the cattle, men coughed and spat to clear their nostrils and throats of the choking clouds of dust. Their trail boss rode ahead of the herd, occasionally glancing over his shoulder to check the drive's progress.

Drovers and cattle rounded the town on its western side and then headed straight for the river. Gabe was riding the flank position on the eastern side of the herd. Dillworth was some yards ahead of him, and on his opposite side the chuck wagon rumbled along. Behind the wagon came the wrangler with his remuda.

The point men on either side of the herd ahead of Gabe moved in on the cattle, narrowing the drift as they did so. Gabe did the same and as he did, the lead steer at the head of the herd went into the red-brown water followed by the cattle tightly bunched behind it. Within seconds, the first of the longhorns were in the deep water which was the result of the previous night's heavy rain.

Curly, riding point directly ahead of Gabe turned in his saddle and yelled, "Look at those so-and-so's! They swim like they think they're swans!"

A moment later, Curly had moved his horse into the water and was swimming it along beside the bulky bodies of the first of the longhorns that had moved into the river.

Within minutes, Gabe was also in the river. He continued working the drift to keep the cows from going anywhere but straight ahead to the bank on the far side which formed the southern border of Chickasaw Nation.

The water was cold. Gabe attributed that to the fact that the snows had probably not completely melted in the mountains where the river had its headwater. When the sun rose higher in the sky, the water would probably warm up. But by that time he fully expected to be out of the river and well into Chickasaw territory.

Such proved not to be the case. Curly was the first drover to spot the trouble.

"They're sinking!" he shouted at the top of his voice.

Ahead of him, Dillworth turned in his saddle and yelled, "What the hell are you talking about, Curly?"

But Curly had no need to answer the trail boss' question. Dillworth was able to see for himself that two of the longhorns had stopped and were standing almost immobile in the river, only their horned heads moving. One of them threw its muzzle up into the air and let out an eerie groan, a kind of pained ululation, that set Gabe's teeth on edge because he knew what had caused it. He knew what the steer was feeling.

Fear.

The animal had become mired in a patch of quicksand for which Red River was infamous. It couldn't move and probably knew on some instinctive level that it was suddenly in grave danger of losing its life.

As the longhorn continued to groan and moan, its eyes wide with fright, the cattle behind it pushed against it. Some of them circled the two mired steers. Others tried to turn back. A few of them made it back to the river's southern bank.

Dillworth yelled, "Drive the herd around those two!"

As his men began to follow the order, one of them returned to the bank on the Texas side of the river to round up the cattle that had climbed out of the water. Gabe rode out of the river and up to the chuck wagon which stood waiting on the Texas side to follow the last of the herd into the river.

"Rope them!" Dillworth shouted, pointing to the two steers that were still mired in the treacherous quicksand. "Pull them out!"

Two of the drovers riding drag on the southern bank left off herding and threw their lariats over the horns of the two endangered steers and then, riding south, they tried to pull them free of the death trap the animals had unwittingly stumbled into.

"Hold it!" Gabe yelled. "You can't get them out that way!"

"You know a better way, Conrad?" one of the two men snapped as he struggled to remain in the saddle and keep his grip on the lariat he was using to try to haul one of the steers out of the sucking quicksand.

"Come with me!" Gabe yelled. He grabbed the coil of rope that hung from his saddle horn and leaped to the ground. "Bring some rope."

When they didn't move, he repeated his order and was relieved to see the two drag riders dismount, take rope from the bed of the chuck wagon, and follow him down to the river.

Hip deep in the water, he bent down beside one of the mired animals. He burrowed with his hands in the quicksand, fighting as he did so to avoid becoming caught in it himself.

The two trail hands splashed into the water beside him.

"Tie their legs," he ordered. "Like this."

He pulled one of the steer's legs free of the quicksand, bent it backward at the knee, and then upward. He tied it tightly in place.

He took his knife and cut the rope, moved around in front of the steer, and began to tie the animal's other front leg as he had just done the first.

"Tie their legs up like I just did—all four of them," he said. "Their legs are like anchors in this muck. But if you can get them tied and the beeves lying on their bellies, they won't sink so fast. Then we'll have a fair to fighting chance of hauling them out of here before they drown."

Following Gabe's instructions, the trail hands set about tying the legs of the second mired steer. As they worked feverishly to save the animals, Gabe climbed out of the river and ran to the chuck wagon.

"Turn this thing around!" he ordered the cook who was sitting on the driver's seat facing the river.

"What for?" the cook asked with a grin. "I've already been back that way. I'm figuring on going forward where there's sights I've never seen before."

Gabe swore and climbed up beside the cook, forcing the man to jump down to the ground. He took the reins and guided the wagon's team until he had the rear of the wagon facing the river. Then he jumped down and called out to the wrangler.

"Give me a hand over here!"

When the wrangler had joined them, Gabe told the boy what he wanted him to do.

The cook protested. "You'll bust up my wagon for good and all if you try that! Don't lay even a little finger on it!"

Gabe ignored the cook. He and the wrangler lifted down the water barrel strapped to the side of the wagon, emptied it, and set it on the ground. Then both men put their shoulders against the wagon and tilted it away from them until the wheels on their side were suspended in the air.

"Prop your water barrel under here!" Gabe yelled over his shoulder to the cook.

When the man had reluctantly obeyed the command, Gabe and the wrangler stepped back from the wagon.

"Now grab hold of the end of one of those lariats," Gabe ordered the wrangler, "and bring it on over here."

When the boy had brought him the lariat, the other end of which was fastened around the horns of one of the mired steers, Gabe quickly tied it tightly to the hub of the larger rear wheel of the chuck wagon.

"Now let's turn this wheel," he said to the wrangler. "You push it toward me, and I'll pull it forward."

Using the suspended wheel as a capstan, Gabe and the wrangler slowly turned the wheel, gradually dragging the steer at the other end of the rope safely out of the river.

Gabe quickly removed the rope from the wheel's hub, grabbed the end of another rope, and repeated the process, freeing the second steer.

Gabe beckoned to the wrangler, and the two of them removed the water barrel from under the tilted chuck wagon and righted it.

Gabe then removed his hat and, using his sleeve, wiped the sweat from his face. Then he freed the legs of the steers he and the drag riders had tied. When he was finished, he stared out over the river to where longhorns were climbing the northern bank and shaking the water from their hides. There were still scores of steers in the river as they made the crossing, their horns and upturned noses the only things rising above the surface of the swiftly flowing river as they swam it on their way to solid ground. No more steers had become mired in the quicksand.

"That was some job you did," the cook commented as he climbed back up on his chuck wagon. "Never did see anybody pull a trick like that there one before. Of course, a lot of the credit goes to my chuck wagon, I think you'll agree."

With that wry comment, the cook clucked to his team and proceeded to drive his chuck wagon into the river. It rolled and heaved as it battled the current, but it arrived safely on the Chickasaw side where Dillworth was sitting his saddle and waving.

"The boss wants us to herd the rest of these critters across," said one of the drag riders who had helped Gabe free the two steers from the quicksand. "We'll drive 'em downriver away from the quicksand around here and hope there's none to be found down in that direction."

Gabe joined the man and the other drag rider. The three of them spent the better part of the next hour getting the last of the herd safely across the river and into Chickasaw Nation.

Just beyond the bank of the river stood a forest of post and blackjack oaks. Its depths struck Gabe as a perfect symbol of the territory they had just entered—dark and vaguely threatening, but apparently peaceful.

So far.

"Get 'em up and move 'em out!" Dillworth bellowed, waving his arm and pointing north.

As the trail boss turned his horse and rode in among the towering oaks, Gabe and the other drovers got the cattle, many of which had dropped down on the ground to their feet, and sent them plodding after Dillworth who was already lost to sight amid the thick shadows under the oaks.

Two days later, as the sun was hanging low in the sky, Gabe, saddle-sore and wishing he would never again have to set his eyes on a Texas longhorn, saw a carriage coming toward him from behind the herd. It was being drawn by a matched pair of chestnut horses with manes like silk and coats that glistened in the day's late light.

But it was not the fine horseflesh or the richly appointed carriage with the molded black rubber roof that had attracted his attention. It was instead the young woman seated in it beside the elderly, bewhiskered man who was driving the rig.

The man drove through the dust the herd was raising as it plodded northward. The woman in the carriage glanced at Gabe who was riding flank position, and he touched the brim of his hat to her. She looked away. He didn't. She looked back at him. He smiled. She didn't.

She's not much older than twenty, twenty-one, he speculated as he spurred his buckskin to keep pace with the wagon that was traveling parallel to the herd. Her hair was black and arranged rather severely—parted in the middle and drawn back in a bun at the nape of her neck. Her eyes were also black and her skin dusky. She's Chickasaw, he thought, or I miss my guess. From what he could see, she had a fine figure. Her body was slender but not gaunt. Her breasts were very definitely there but not buxom.

"Good day to you," he said as he rode beside the carriage.

The elderly man returned his greeting in a gruff voice. The woman said nothing. Her eyes were suddenly intent upon the beaded reticule she held in her folded hands which rested demurely in her lap.

"You folks live around here, do you?" Gabe inquired politely.

"Near enough," was the man's cryptic reply. He slapped the rumps of his chestnuts with his reins. The carriage picked up speed, outdistancing Gabe who had to remain with the herd.

"Pleased to make your acquaintances," he said softly and with faint annoyance as he tipped his hat to the rear of the departing carriage.

"You win some and you lose a lot, if you're at all like me," Dave Carmody said as he rode up from behind the herd to join Gabe. "Not bad-looking, was she?"

"Not bad at all."

"It's been so long since I had me a female, some of these cows are starting to look good," Carmody said and cackled. "Maybe if Mr. Dillworth lets us bed down near some Chickasaw town, I'll be able to satisfy the urge I've got. Indian women have a yearning for white men, so they say."

Gabe warned himself to remain calm. He set about deliberately clamping a lid on his rising temper. Carmody's words had infuriated him. They were typical of the way some—far too many, in his opinion—white men viewed Indian women. Chattel, that's all they were to such white men. Or worse. Whores, for example. He knew that was how some white men wanted Indian women to be. They imagined an Indian woman would flop down on her back at the slightest gesture or word from men like themselves.

Gabe knew that, on the contrary, the women of most tribes were generally chaste. Oh, he knew there were adulteresses among them, but they were far outnumbered by their more modest sisters. He said nothing about his thoughts to Carmody. He knew they would not alter the man's way of thinking, and they just might raise questions in Carmody's mind about how Gabe knew so much about the behavior of Indian women. Questions Gabe would prefer not to answer—or even have raised in the first place. So he said nothing.

"Mr. Dillworth must have gotten lost," Carmody mused, changing the subject as they rode along together. "He went out on the scout for water hours ago, and I haven't seen hide nor hair of him since, have you?"

"No, he's not come back yet."

"If these beeves don't get some water soon, we're going to have trouble with them. We haven't hit a stream or even a crick since we left Red River. Which was the last time these cattle have had a chance to slake their thirst. And that was two days ago."

They rode along in silence for a time. The silence was broken by Carmody. "See? What'd I tell you? Didn't I tell you we were in for trouble with these cattle? They're getting restless. They're going to run, if you ask me. Either north or south, depending on whether they can smell water up ahead or they've made up their minds to head back to where they remember there's water—the Red River."

Gabe rode up and drove several steers who had left the drift back into the herd. He knew Carmody was right. Cows kept too long from water could turn cantankerous fast.

"Here comes Mr. Dillworth now," he said as he rejoined Carmody.

Both men watched as the trail boss rode up to the front of the herd and signaled for a halt. For the next several minutes, the drovers busied themselves stopping the herd. Dillworth ordered Curly and another drover to ride loose herd to keep them from ranging too far afield.

"There's water about two miles up ahead of here," Dillworth announced. "Only trouble is it's fouled by alkali deposits. I rode on beyond it and east and west of it, but I couldn't find another source of water anywhere. We won't hit sweet water, it looks like, till we reach the Washita River."

"That's a pretty far piece from here, Mr. Dillworth," Curly noted.

"Damn it, don't you think I know that?" snapped Dillworth. "But we can't let them drink the alkaline water that lies up ahead. They're going to have to wait to slake their thirsts till we reach the Washita."

"Pardon me, Mr. Dillworth," one of the trail hands said hesitantly, "but how the hell are we going to stop a herd this size from drinking that bad water you found?"

"There's only one way to stop them from drinking," Dillworth replied. "We're going to have to deliberately stampede them through the water so they don't have time to drink."

The drovers exchanged concerned glances. Every man present knew the dangers associated with stampedes, no matter how they started. To deliberately start one . . .

"I know what you men are thinking," Dillworth said as if he had read his drovers' thoughts. "But it's either stampede the herd or lose a bunch of them to that filthy water. I don't take too kindly to the latter choice, I can tell you that.

"So let's get to it, men. Keep the cattle under a tight hold right up until we get to the riverbank. When we do, when the moment's right, I'll give the signal, and then you all

run those cows through and well beyond the water like you
were the Devil himself and they were sinful souls you were
out to round up. Move 'em out!"

The drovers proceeded to throw the herd on the trail
again. There was apprehension in more than one pair of
eyes as they did so. They soon had the herd drifting north,
and they had not gone far when the steers began to quicken
their pace.

Curly, riding some distance behind Gabe, called out,
"They can smell it, the water. Look at 'em go, will you?"

The leaders of the drift had begun to run. The others, after
only a moment's bewildered hesitation, began to follow
them. Dust rose in an almost impenetrable cloud, partially
obscuring the running longhorns.

The drovers moved in close to them. They got a grip on
their coiled lariats or their rain slickers as they waited for
the trail boss to give them the signal they were all nervously
waiting for.

Gabe had his slicker in his left hand. He guided his buckskin with only knee pressure and an occasional light touch
of his spurs. The horse responded well. It trotted close to the
herd, its body at times nearly bumping up against the steers
which caused Gabe to get ready to throw his left leg over
his saddle horn to protect it. But such a maneuver proved to
be unnecessary. He was able to keep the buckskin close but
not dangerously close to the running longhorns. He pulled
his bandanna up to cover his nose and mouth. It afforded
him some protection from the roiling dust, but some of it
still found its way beneath the bandanna and into his nose
and mouth.

He could barely make out the mounted figure of Dillworth
in the distance ahead of him. The man was riding just to the
right of the advancing herd, his eyes fixed straight ahead.
Gabe watched him stand up in his stirrups and then gallop
onward. The cattle seemed to be in a race with him. They
ran nearly as fast as Dillworth's horse.

Minutes later, Dillworth once again stood up in his stirrups. This time he turned and, taking off his hat, waved it
in a wide arc.

The drovers all responded by leaning over in their saddles and popping their slickers in the faces of the cattle. Others did the same with their lariats. Gabe's slicker caught and tore on the horns of one of the steers as he flailed it about to keep the herd running at an even faster pace than the one they were presently pursuing.

The drovers shouted at the cattle. They kicked out at them.

The longhorns responded by racing at a fast clip toward the riverbank that lay directly ahead. If they thought that there they would find relief from the tormenting maneuvers of the drovers, they were wrong. The drovers rode right into the water alongside the steers. Their yellow slickers flashed in the sun's light that was turning orange now. Their lariats made harsh slapping sounds as they struck flesh.

A thick spray flew up into the air as the cattle plowed through the water. The spray sparkled in the light of the sun and showered both the steers that were causing it and the drovers herding them. Water struck Gabe full in the face. He blinked it away and continued forcing the cattle onward through the swift current. The cattle, despite their thirst, were responding now to a primeval emotion—fear. They feared the drovers' slickers and lariats that fell upon them relentlessly.

Within five minutes the first of the steers were up and out of the water on the opposite bank. Those following behind forced their companions to move away from the riverbank. A loud bawling went up from the cattle on the far bank of the river as they began to slow down and then stopped. Some of them turned around and headed back toward the water.

Gabe cut them off. He rode straight at them, whirling his slicker above his head and shouting at the top of his voice, "Ho ho ho cattle *ho!*" They skidded to a startled halt before he reached them and then peeled away, some of them heading one way, some the other. He went after the first group, caught up with them, slashed the face of their ringleader with his slicker, and sent them thudding back the way they had come. When they had caught up with the other group that was heading again for the water, Gabe put spurs to his buckskin and circled around in front of them. Again, using his slicker as a kind of weapon, he managed to stop them in their tracks and send them in the direction the other drovers were driving the rest of the herd—north.

The battle between drovers and steers went on past sunset and long into the night as steers bolted from the drift and tried to return to the water that lay behind them. Throughout the area, men could be heard calling to and cursing the cattle. The thudding of hooves drowned out the plaintive cries of night birds.

Gabe rode out after a group of six steers that had broken away from the main drift which the other drovers were trying desperately to keep moving north and disappeared in the darkness. He could hear them thrashing through a thicket up ahead of him but couldn't see them. He gave his horse free rein and raked it with his spurs. Dodging past tangled stands of chokecherry bushes, he continued his pursuit of the renegade steers.

Sweat dripped from his face and soaked his shirt as he rode even though the night was cool. The sound of the fleeing longhorns faded and then stopped altogether. Gabe slowed his buckskin and squinted at the dim ground in front of him. He rode slowly now, trying to follow the tracks of the escaped steers. They were clear enough but still hard to see in the darkness. He lost the trail completely for a time when it led him into a growth of scrub oak where he could barely see his hand in front of his face.

He emerged from the trees onto a savannah that stretched for miles in every direction. There, in the middle of the tableland were the steers he had been pursuing. They were standing with their heads lowered as they calmly and quietly browsed the buffalo grass covering the prairie.

With a sigh, Gabe set out after them. He had not gone far when he spotted the log cabin half-hidden behind a hummock which offered it protection from north winds. Someone had planted a windbreak on the eastern side of the cabin and maybe that same someone was the one who had built the sturdy outbuildings—the tack shed, the outhouse, and the barn.

Yellow lamplight brightened the windows in the front of the cabin. Smoke rose from a stone chimney.

Gabe was about fifty yards from the cabin on his way to gather up the steers he was after when he saw a woman emerge from the barn, a lantern in her hand.

In the faint light of the lantern he immediately recognized the woman he had seen earlier in the day riding in the carriage with the elderly man. He turned his horse and rode toward her.

When she saw him coming, she halted. He could see the expression of unease—no, fear—on her lovely face as he came closer.

He called out, "I mean you no harm, ma'am. I'm on my way to round up that bunch of steers over yonder."

She said nothing as he drew rein beside her.

With his hands folded around his saddle horn, he studied her. The lantern light gave her smooth skin a rich glow. Her black eyes sparkled in it. It gave a sheen to her black hair.

"My name's Gabe Conrad," he told her, talking softly as one would to an animal one didn't want to spook. "You saw me earlier today. I'm with the cattle drive you passed by in your carriage."

"Yes," she said, her voice barely audible.

"This your home place, is it?"

"It is."

"You live here with your daddy, do you?"

"My father's dead. So is my mother. I live here with my grandfather. His name's Harley Sadler. I'm Annie Sadler."

"Miss Sadler, I hate to trouble you at this time of night, but I sure would appreciate it if you'd let me draw a drink of water from your well for me and my horse."

"Oh, why of course. Please help yourself."

Gabe dismounted and, as he passed Annie on his way to the well, she drew back from him. He lowered the oaken bucket into the well and then cranked it up. He used the metal dipper resting on the circular stone lip of the well to drink from. When he had drunk his fill, he poured water into his hat and held it out for his horse to drink from.

"We're both parched," he told Annie while his buckskin made loud sloshing noises as it eagerly drank. "We've been out here chasing after those steers that ran off, and I have to admit we're not just thirsty, we're both pretty close to tuckered."

"Are you going to Abilene?"

"No, ma'am, we're headed for Dodge City." Gabe, as his horse stopped drinking, shook the little remaining water out of his hat and clapped it back on his head.

"I've heard tell that Dodge City is an exciting town," Annie said, a faraway look in her eyes. "I've never been there, of course."

"Most Kansas cow towns are pretty lively."

"You have your permit, I suppose."

"Permit?"

"From the Chickasaw authorities. To allow you to pass through the Nation."

"That's a new wrinkle as I understand it. The last time I was here, herds were moving through just as free as you please."

"Some of those herds spread Texas fever," Annie said. "That's one of the reasons our tribal council instituted the practice of requiring permits. In the process of issuing them, the authorities can check the herds for the fever."

Annie walked a few steps away from Gabe and stood with her hands clasped in front of her as she stared up at the now starry sky above the hummock looming near the cabin.

"A penny for your thoughts, Annie."

She started. "Oh, I was just thinking about—things. I sometimes sit up there on that hill and think about all the places there are in the world. The fine and pleasant places, like Dodge City."

Gabe refrained from expressing the thought that leaped to the forefront of his mind as a result of her words.

Dodge City, as far as he was concerned, was far from fine or pleasant. Rowdy was the word that fit it better.

"I sometimes watch the cattle herds passing along the Chisholm Trail from up there, and I always find myself envying the drovers. Men are so fortunate. They can go where and when they please. Women, on the other hand, are bound by so many conventions which I, for one, find quite constricting."

"Maybe you'll get to visit Dodge some day and see for yourself what it's like. Sometimes the dream doesn't match up with the reality."

Annie gave a little laugh. "Oh, I doubt that I'll ever get as far as Dodge. Why, I've never even been to Ardmore, and that's the closest thing to a city around here."

"I'm obliged to you for the water, Annie."

She turned back to face him as he swung into the saddle. "I hope you'll have a safe trip. I hope the Lighthorsemen don't give you any difficulty."

"You're talking about the Chickasaw police."

She nodded. "Good-bye, Mr. Conrad."

Gabe touched the brim of his hat to her and rode away, heading for the six head of cattle in the distance. When he had them started in the direction he wanted to go, he looked back over his shoulder.

Annie was still standing outside the cabin she shared with her grandfather. She was watching him. When he waved to her, she shyly waved back before entering the cabin and closing the door behind her.

"Ho cattle," Gabe said, but his heart wasn't in it. Thoughts of the lovely Annie ran rampant in his mind.

But by the time he had gotten the six steers back to where the herd was moving in a nervous mill, he had almost managed to put her out of his mind.

"That's the last of them, men," Dillworth called out as Gabe folded his six steers into the herd. "Conrad, we're getting out of here. If we don't, we're going to lose these beeves to that poisoned water we left behind us."

"You're fixing to drive them all night?" an incredulous Gabe inquired.

"I am." There was a note of belligerence in Dillworth's voice. "We'll ride tight herd on them until we can get them up to the Washita River."

"That'll take till at least some time tomorrow, Boss," one of the drovers commented.

"I don't care if it takes till the Last Judgment. That's what we're going to do. I know we're running weight off them this way. But skinny steers are better than steers lost to bad water, in my book.

"As it is, they're not far from being scrub stock, the way we've been driving them. If I had my way, we wouldn't drive them at all. The thing to do with cows on the trail is to *move* them, not drive them. But this world's not a perfect place, and I've done what I had to do and intend to keep on doing the same damn thing.

"But once we get to the Washita, we'll stop for a spell. A few days of rest ought to put some meat back on the bones of these beeves. There's good grass on the river's bottomland and plenty of water. I know we'll lose trail time. But what it all comes down to in the end is having to choose between the lesser of two evils. And that's just exactly what I've done."

"Mr. Dillworth—"

"Move 'em out, men!" Dillworth bellowed, drowning out Gabe's words. He rode out to the front of the herd and trotted north as the drovers began to move the restless cattle in the same direction.

Gabe never got a chance to mention to Dillworth the matter of permits that Annie Sadler had told him about.

CHAPTER FIVE

They arrived at the Washita River just after noon on the following day after a sleepless night of riding herd. Which meant struggling to keep the drift in line and having to ride out time after time to bring back runaway steers who were still trying to make it back to the alkaline water they had been stampeded through to keep them from drinking it.

Gabe sat his saddle and stared out over the herd that was spread now over a vast expense of rich bottomland thick with tall grama grass. Strung like a silver ribbon through the savannah was the wide Washita, flowing in a smooth southeasterly course. The sun glistened on its surface, and the river was dotted with steers standing hock deep in it as if they never intended to leave the sweet water they had at last reached.

Gabe jerked his head up, suddenly conscious of the fact that he had fallen asleep in the saddle. He glanced over to where Dillworth was hunkered down beside the fire the cook had built near the chuck wagon. The trail boss seemed not to have noticed his momentary lapse.

When it happened a second time, he rode over to where Curly was riding slowly along the herd's southern perimeter. "Have you got any tobacco?" he asked the drover.

"Sure, I have. But I didn't think you smoked." Curly pulled the round tag hanging from his vest pocket and out came a muslin sack of Bull Durham which carried a picture of a bull on its front side.

Gabe took it from him and extracted a pinch of tobacco which he placed in his right eye. Then he placed another small pinch in his left eye. The strong sting of the tobacco made both of his eyes water.

"What are you trying to do, blind yourself?" a concerned Curly asked.

"No. It's just a trick I learned from an old-timer who spent most of his life on the cow trails. Tobacco in the eyes is guaranteed to keep a man wide awake in or out of the saddle. Unless it stings him to death first."

"I reckon that stuff smarts."

"You reckon right." Gabe handed the sack back to Curly. "I'm much obliged to you." He rode back to his former position and this time he did not nod off as tears, brought to his eyes by the tobacco, coursed down his cheeks.

Through them the cattle shimmered wetly. The river danced.

He squeezed his eyes shut, willing the pain away, and then opened them to see five mounted men riding into the cow camp, all of them armed, all of them uniformed. He knew at once he was watching the approach of a contingent of Chickasaw Lighthorsemen.

Annie Sadler's words about the need for a permit to cross Chickasaw land echoed in his mind. He spurred his buckskin and rode over to where Dillworth, out of the saddle now, was watching, with hands planted on hips, the approach of the Indian policemen.

"Mr. Dillworth," Gabe began when he reached the trail boss, "I tried to tell you before—"

"Who's in charge of this herd?" one of the Lighthorsemen asked as he and the men with him drew rein not far from where Dillworth and Gabe were standing.

"I am," Dillworth answered and gave his name. "Who wants to know?"

"My name's Jackson Wolf," said the man who had just spoken. "I'm with the Chickasaw Lighthorsemen as are these men with me. This is your herd?"

"Of course it's my herd," Dillworth answered testily. "What did you think? That me and my men had rustled it?"

Wolf's face remained impassive. His eyes, black as a moonless and starless night, gazed steadily at Dillworth. "You've got papers to prove these longhorns belong to you?"

"They don't belong to me, strictly speaking," Dillworth said, rummaging about in the pocket of the leather jacket he was wearing. "I mean to say that I'm driving them to Dodge City for a bunch of their owners. You can see for yourself they bear all sorts of different brands, but if you look close you'll see that they bear a trail brand as well."

"I see that," Wolf said tonelessly.

"Here," Dillworth said, handing the leader of the Lighthorsemen a folded wad of paper. "Before I left Texas, the owners of these animals gave me these bills of sale for them so that I'd have legal proof that what I've told you is the truth."

Wolf accepted the papers Dillworth was holding up to him, unfolded them, and began to read.

Gabe studied the man as he did so. Wolf was taller than most Chickasaws. Gabe guessed that he was pushing six feet. Had maybe even topped it. It was hard to tell for sure how tall a man he was when he was mounted as Wolf was. He had the high and prominent cheekbones of an Indian and the black hair and eyes of that race. But his skin was lighter than most Indians, far lighter than members of tribes such as the Sioux or Comanche. Gabe suspected that there was some white blood flowing in Jackson Wolf's veins. He knew that many of the members of the five so-called "civilized tribes" had intermarried with whites back East where they had originally come from.

He recalled some of the stories he had heard about the long and arduous—and in some cases fatal—journey west by the five tribes, taken as a result of an order of the United States government. They had been forced to leave the southern United States that had been their home for generations and head west in winter, leaving behind them the fine homes they had built and all the property they had, by diligent labor and thrift, managed to acquire.

Gabe had heard of the many deaths that had occurred during that bitter journey which the tribes had come to call, with justification, the "Trail of Tears." Many of the old and the very young had died on that journey, broken by blizzards and the memories of white people looting their ancestral homes even before they, their owners, were out of sight of them.

Gabe continued studying the man as Wolf refolded the papers in his hands and returned them to Dillworth, the breeze sweeping across the savannah ruffling his straight black hair which fell below the collar of his shirt.

"I am satisfied that you have a right to the cattle you're herding" Wolf said. "Have you obtained a permit to cross Chickasaw land, Mr. Dillworth?"

"A permit?" Dillworth's face wore an incredulous expression. "I don't have any notion of what you're talking about."

"The Nation has established the practice of requiring permits for Texas herds to cross our land. I take it you have not bothered to obtain one."

"I didn't know such a thing was required. Last time I traveled the Chisholm Trail across your territory no such problem ever presented itself."

"I can issue you a permit for twenty-five dollars," Wolf said.

"Twenty-five dollars!" Carmody exclaimed from where he was standing and listening to the conversation a few feet away. "Mr. Dillworth, that's highway robbery!"

Dillworth was silent for a moment. Then he said, "I'm inclined to agree with you, Dave."

"It might be a good idea to buy a permit," Gabe said in a low voice to Dillworth who was, he could see, silently fuming as he locked eyes with Wolf. "Twenty-five dollars is a small price to pay for peace. And this is, after all, Chickasaw land."

"We have had difficulty for some time with Texas herds and their drovers," Wolf said. "They have been using our grass without recompense, intruding on our domain without our permission, and generally making a nuisance of themselves. We—that is to say, the tribal council—had seen fit to impose the permit system in order to obtain some measure of control over who may use our land and resources and under what conditions."

"You talk about your domain," Dillworth spat. "You people are on this land by sufferance of the United States government. I don't see where you get off making up rules and regulations to cause grief for men like me."

"There are treaties," Wolf said quietly, "agreements made in good faith by both sides."

"If I pay the twenty-five dollars you're trying to gouge out of me, does that mean me and my men will be left alone?"

"Of course, Mr. Dillworth." A pause. "After we inspect your cattle for Texas fever. I've brought with me our stock superintendent to inspect your herd. His name is William Colbert."

Dillworth glanced at the straight-backed Indian Wolf had pointed out. "What makes you think my herd's got the fever?"

"We don't think it," Wolf replied. "We just want to make sure your animals are healthy to protect our own herds from disease."

"How much is this inspection of yours going to cost me?"

"Not a cent, Mr. Dillworth," Wolf answered. "But if your herd is found to be infected, it will be escorted under armed guard back to Texas."

"Well, I'll be damned!" Carmody exploded. "Listen to that redskin talk, will you? He talks like he owns the world and all that's in it."

Gabe tensed. He could sense trouble coming down the trail.

"By what goddamned authority do you come barging into this cow camp of mine and start telling me what I have to do and not do?" Dillworth asked in a voice that was as cold as an icehouse.

"I'm a duly appointed officer representing Chickasaw Nation," Wolf said, just as coldly. Then, turning to the man next to him, he said, "Check the herd, Colbert."

"You'll check no herd of mine!" Dillworth practically shouted as he stepped forward and seized Colbert's bridle to keep the rider from moving out.

"You're looking for trouble, mister," Colbert warned him. "You can't stop me from inspecting your beeves."

"I am stopping you," Dillworth insisted. "You ought to be able to see that."

Colbert shook a foot free of his stirrups and then kicked Dillworth's hand, breaking the trail boss' grip on his bridle. Before Dillworth could make another move, Colbert clucked to his horse and rode out.

"Stop him!" Dillworth shouted.

His drovers, with the single exception of Gabe, headed for Colbert who had dismounted and was beginning to check the cattle for signs of fever.

"Hold it!" Wolf's six-gun cleared leather and took direct aim at Dillworth.

The drovers froze.

"That's better," Wolf said. "Anybody makes a move to interfere with the stock superintendent, he'll do so knowing that the consequences of his action will be, to say the least, severe."

Carmody moved up to stand beside Dillworth.

"He sure has got a high-handed way about him, ain't he, Boss?" Carmody muttered, his eyes on the gun in Wolf's hand.

Dillworth said nothing as he slowly turned to watch Colbert moving about among his herd.

No one spoke while the stock superintendent continued his inspection. When at last it had finally been completed and Colbert had climbed back into the saddle and returned to his place beside Wolf, he reported, "They're clean, Jackson. There's no sign of anything wrong with them other than a couple cases of lump jaw I spotted and a lot of cripples suffering sore feet."

"I could have told you that," a furious Dillworth snarled.

"It wouldn't have done you any good had you done so," Wolf remarked. "Mr. Colbert would still have had to make an up-close inspection."

"Well, now that he has, you and your men can clear out of here," Dillworth said. "We have work to do, and you're holding us up."

"There are one or two more matters that need to be mentioned," Wolf said almost, but not quite, amiably.

"What matters?" Dillworth asked, his brow furrowing.

"You're not allowed to keep your cows spread out the way they are at the moment. You're allowed to graze them for a distance of only one mile on either side of the Chisholm Trail you're following."

"What the hell are you talking about?" Carmody bellowed at Wolf. "There's not enough grass in that little bit of space to feed a flock of hungry geese let alone hundreds of cows."

"That is the law," Wolf stated flatly. "Grazing is permitted, I repeat, for a mile on either side of the Trail. And then only upon payment of fifteen cents an animal."

Dillworth let out a wordless roar of protest. He took off his hat and slapped it against his thigh, looking as if he wanted to kill Wolf on the spot. He rammed his hat back on his head and stood there spluttering under Wolf's still-drawn gun.

"Another thing," the leader of the Lighthorsemen said. "The law requires that you keep your herd moving through the Nation at a rate of no less than eight miles a day."

"Now you just wait one minute here!" Dillworth exploded. "To hear you talk, me and my men and my cows have to dance to all kinds of tunes you've taken a notion to playing. We've had ourselves a hard time on the trail up until now. We had a stampede back in Texas in which we lost more head than I care to count. Then we had to stampede the cattle ourselves to get them past some alkaline water that would have killed them if they'd had a chance to taste it.

"They've lost a lot of flesh as you can plainly see, and that means if I deliver them to the buyers in Dodge looking like the scrub they presently are, their owners are going to lose money on them. If that happens, my reputation as a knowledgeable trail boss is bound to suffer. As a result, I might not get another herd to drive. I won't get a chance to work at what I do best."

"Eight miles a day," Wolf repeated. "Minimum."

"Don't let him buffalo you, Boss," Carmody urged.

Dillworth's face turned red as he inwardly raged.

Gabe said, addressing the trail boss, "We could graze them good once we get them across the border into Kansas. If we travel eight miles a day—if we were to push it and try for ten to fifteen—we'd be across into Kansas by—"

"No!"

The word Dillworth roared had sounded like a minor explosion.

"No!" the trail boss repeated, vigorously shaking his head. "I won't do it! You can take your rules and regulations, Wolf, and shove them where the sun doesn't shine!"

"We'll give you a day to comply, Mr. Dillworth. We'll be back here the same time tomorrow. We'll have a permit ready for you at that time which will allow you to cross Chickasaw land. You have the twenty-five dollars it costs ready to hand over at that time. Also the fifteen cents per-head payment for grazing rights you'll be permitted within the restrictions of space and time I have just outlined for you. Is that understood?"

Dillworth didn't answer. Instead, he turned and stalked away. A moment later, Carmody followed him.

Wolf holstered his gun and rode away. The stock superintendent and the other Lighthorsemen followed him.

"If that bunch shows up here tomorrow like they say they mean to, we ought to lynch them all from the same tree," Carmody declared that night as the drovers and Dillworth gathered around the cook's fire to eat their supper.

Several of the drovers grunted their approval of the suggestion as they forked food into their mouths.

"I'm not a violent man," Dillworth said, "but the way that Jackson Wolf went about things, it makes me see red, I can tell you."

"What are you fixing to do, Boss?" Curly inquired.

"I don't know for sure at this point. I never ran into a situation like this one before. But I can tell you one thing. I won't be run off like some damned dog with my tail tucked between my legs."

"We'll stand by you, Boss," Curly assured Dillworth.

The trail boss put his plate down on the ground and looked from one to the other of the men surrounding him, Gabe among them. "There's something that's been sticking in my craw ever since those Lighthorsemen showed up here this afternoon."

"What's that, Boss?" Carmody asked.

"The way I see it, I've got no right to put any of you men in danger. Not the kind Wolf and his men represent, I mean. It's one thing to face up to foul weather and stampedes and accidents on the trail. When a man signs on a drive, he knows he's likely to run into one or more of those problems before he's through. It's another thing altogether to ask drovers to step into the middle of what might well become a shooting war."

"Like Curly said, Boss," Carmody said, "we'll stand by you. There's not a man among us'll turn tail and run. Ain't that right, boys?"

There were murmurs of agreement from the men.

"We outnumber them," Carmody pointed out. "We've got the numbers on our side."

"Unless Wolf brings reinforcements with him when he shows up here tomorrow," Dillworth mused gloomily.

"We'll be ready for him," Carmody declared confidently. "Ain't no ragtag bunch of Injuns going to tell us what to do. This here's a free country."

"This is their country, Carmody," Gabe interjected. "Let's not lose sight of that fact."

"Their country, hell!" Carmody snarled. "What it amounts to is this land's a reservation the government of the United States put those savages on to keep them out of everybody's hair."

"Only now they're in our hair," Curly offered.

"As I understand it," Gabe said, forcing himself to be calm, "the superintendent of the five civilized tribes, as

folks have taken to calling them, sets the rules and regulations for the Nations along with the tribal council. That's
the same thing as saying the United States government itself
did it."

"This here superintendent," Carmody said, "is he a white
man or an Injun?"

"He's white." What the hell difference does it make,
Gabe wanted to ask Carmody, but he didn't.

"Imagine that," Carmody muttered, shaking his head. "A
white man letting a bunch of ignorant savages order other
white men around. Giving them guns to do it with, too. It's
a damn disgrace, that's what it is."

"Those Injun policemen," one of the other drovers began
tentatively, "they looked, some of them did, almost white,
did anybody notice?"

"I noticed," Curly volunteered.

"Their men must have gotten under more than a few
white women's skirts," Carmody muttered. "Damned animals. They ought to be kept penned up."

One of the drovers giggled. "Maybe it was the other way
around, Dave."

"What are you talking about?" Carmody asked.

"Maybe it was the white women that got into the Indian
buck's pants."

"Dammit, that's no way to talk about white women!"
Carmody practically shouted. "No white woman would do
a thing like that. She wouldn't dare! Folks find out about it,
they'd tar and feather her and run her out of polite society
on a rail."

"Mr. Dillworth," Gabe said, "why not just pay the fees
the Chickasaws are asking for and keep things calm?"

The trail boss shook his head. "I won't be buffaloed into
a deal like the one that Wolf offered us. Besides, I'm not
authorized by the owners of the cattle we're driving to make
such expenditures."

"There's another way we might get around this problem
we're facing," Gabe remarked thoughtfully.

Dillworth looked at him, one eyebrow arched. "What
way might that be?"

"We could turn the herd east. Drive them over into Choctaw Nation. We could be there in three days if we kept a steady pace."

"What happens if those other redskins have the same notion of bleeding us dry to let us pass through their territory—or what they're pleased to consider their territory?" Carmody inquired, skepticism giving a sharp edge to his voice.

"He's got a point, Gabe." Curly observed.

Gabe had to concede it. But he was not willing to abandon his proposal entirely. "Suppose they do try to charge us. We could load our herd on cattle cars and ship them up to Kansas on the Missouri, Kansas, and Texas Railroad. That way we'd save a lot of time getting them to Kansas. We could use some of that time we saved to fatten them up on Kansas grass before we herd them west to Dodge."

"I like the idea of saving time," Dillworth said.

Gabe began to think, as a result of the trail boss' statement, that the trouble he was sure was coming could be averted.

But then Dillworth added, "But I've got no money to pay to ship these cattle of ours on any railroad, and it's not likely that their owners will authorize such an expenditure. In fact, I'm sure they won't. They're a tightfisted bunch. To a man, they are."

"Then your only other choice is to give in to what the Chickasaws want," Gabe suggested.

"You're wrong on that score, Conrad. I'm not giving in. I'm going to fight if I have to."

"We all are," Carmody said and looked about for dissent from the drovers gathered around the fire. He got none.

"Better oil your guns tonight, men," Dillworth advised. "If anybody's short of ammunition, somebody share his with that man."

Carmody stood up and stretched, the firelight dancing on his coarse features. "I'm going into that town we passed last night on the way here. I figure it's high time I got myself some sippin' whiskey and a woman and have myself a party before the fight starts tomorrow."

"I hope you'll be back here in time to join it," Dillworth called out as Carmody headed for the remuda.

Carmody turned and waved. "I'll be here, Boss. No need for you to fret on that account. I love a good fight. Wouldn't miss this one for all the tea in China."

Next morning, after a breakfast of fried salt pork, boiled beans, cornbread, and coffee, Dillworth assigned two of his drovers to ride loose herd. "The rest of you men do what you can to get rid of the screwworms that have infested some of the stock and dehorn any steers you find that've got misshapen horns."

Gabe went to the chuck wagon and asked the cook if he had anything that could be used to treat screwworms.

"You came to the right place, Conrad. I've got just the thing for you." The cook pulled open one of the drawers of his chuck box and took out an unlabeled brown glass bottle with a cork stopper. He handed the bottle to Gabe.

"What's this stuff?"

"My own special mixture. In there's a combination of carbolic acid and axle grease. I personally guarantee it'll work. If it doesn't cure the cows, it'll kill 'em. Either way they won't give you any more trouble."

As the cook bent over and slapped his knees, laughing loudly, Gabe took the bottle he had been given and walked down the slight slope to where the herd was peacefully grazing. On the way, he picked up a stick which he intended to use to dispense the mixture contained in the bottle he was carrying. He didn't want to risk touching it since it contained a corrosive acid. He moved cautiously in among the cattle, careful to avoid the steers' long horns which could become lethal weapons.

Within minutes, he had found a cow that was infested with the deadly screwworms which, he knew, caused the animal agonizing pain and could, and did in many cases, ultimately kill the animal. He uncorked the bottle and gingerly poured some of the black viscous mixture it contained onto the end of his stick. It flowed slowly. Like maple syrup in March up north, he thought. When he had the end of the stick covered with salve, he stepped up to the cow and, before she could realize what he was going to do, he daubed the mixture on her open wound that was severly festered.

The cow unappreciative of his efforts to aid her, bawled in outrage and promptly bolted.

Undismayed by her lack of gratitude, Gabe moved on, his eyes roving over the bony bodies of the herd animals as he searched for more infections. The next one he found was on the rump of a steer. The animal had somehow managed to gouge itself, and the resulting wound was infested with blowflies and the eggs those insects had laid in the wound. In a short time, the eggs would hatch into hungry screwworms which would, in their voraciousness, begin to eat the steer alive.

He poured some of the cook's homemade salve on the end of his stick and smeared it on the steer's rump. The caustic substance caused the animal to let out a sound that was somewhere between a bawl and a shriek. It went loping away from Gabe, still loudly protesting its treatment at his hands.

He continued moving through the herd, treating an animal here, dodging a pair of swinging horns there. The stench of the cattle's droppings combined with their own body odors was almost overpowering. He tried his best to ignore it as he continued his makeshift doctoring.

He had worked his way through the herd and was retracing his steps in an effort to discover any cattle he might have missed on his first pass-through when Curly called his name.

He looked over to where Curly was standing with a hack saw in his hand and beckoning to him.

"Barney and me, we could sure use a little help," Curly said as Gabe joined him. He nodded in the direction of the mounted drover who was coiling a grass lariat in his hands. "It's too big a job for the two of us, this dehorning. These steers are more fidgety than a young girl without a gentleman caller on a Saturday night. We can't get the job done, just the two of us. Will you lend us a hand, Gabe?"

"Sure, I will. What exactly do you want me to do?"

"If you'll take my lariat—it's hanging on my saddle horn over there—and rope the back legs of the steers we need to dehorn, Barney can lasso their heads and then the two of you can stretch the steer out on the ground so he'll hold still long enough for me to saw off his horns."

"Be right back." Gabe went to where Curly's horse was standing and removed the drover's rope from the saddle horn. "I'm ready whenever you boys are," he said when he had rejoined Curly and Barney.

"Let's go after that big bastard right there," Curly suggested, pointing out their quarry. "His horns are misshapen all to hell and back. Look at the way they curve backward so sharp. If they grow another two inches—and they will— he'll gore himself every time he turns his head."

Gabe fashioned a honda and ran one end of Curly's rope through it. Then, as Barney whirled his lariat above his head, preparatory to dropping a loop over the steer's head, Gabe took up a position to one side which would allow him to make a heel catch.

He watched Barney as the man's lariat whistled in the air. Only seconds after Barney let go with a long loop, he set Curly's rope to whirling and made a fast toss. Barney's lariat landed on the steer's neck and was immediately pulled taut. Gabe managed a perfect heel catch and wasted no time in pulling the loop tight. At the same time, Barney was reeling in the slack in his lariat.

The steer went down with a bawl of protest and a heavy thud.

Curly moved in on it and placed one knee on the animal's thick neck. Gripping the steer's left horn in one hand, he began to saw into the horn at a spot near the animal's head.

"Watch you don't slice off his ear into the bargain," Barney called out and chuckled.

"You just hold him tight and forget the bad jokes," Curly responded. "If he gets loose, I'm a goner for sure."

Both Gabe and Barney kept their ropes tight, effectively immobilizing the steer. Curly worked on, the rasping of his hacksaw the only sound in the area.

Minutes later, with a sharp cracking sound, the steer's horn split and fell to the ground amid a splatter of blood that sprayed the front of Curly's shirt.

The drover shifted position and got a strong grip on the steer's other horn. While Gabe and Barney held the animal in place, Curly proceeded to saw through that horn. When he had done so, blood spurted from it which missed him this time because he ducked in time.

He leaped to his feet and dropped his saw. He ran over to where a low fire was burning and picked up an iron, one end of which had been in the fire. He ran back to the steer and placed the red-hot end of the iron against first one horn and then the other to cauterize them and stop the bleeding.

The flow of blood slowed to a trickle and then finally stopped altogether.

Curly signaled Gabe and Barney, and both men loosened their lariats and then jerked them free. They had no sooner done so than the steer lumbered to its feet, its hind end rising first and then its front end. Its joints cracked audibly, and then it was gone, racing away into the middle of the herd as if it feared what the three men who had captured it would do to it next.

Curly wiped a sheen of sweat from his forehead. "I wish to hell the fellas who own these cows had dehorned them when they were little ones. All they would have had to do at that point is rub a little caustic potash on their horn buttons during the first week they put in an appearance. That would have kept 'em from growing and saved us a lot of hard work."

"You did him good, Curly," Barney commented. "I reckon if you were to meet up with Lucifer himself one of these days, you could dehorn that old Prince of Darkness faster than a stuttering man can say shucks."

The three men, working as a team, cut another steer out of the herd which also had misshapen horns.

"Rope him real tight," an apprehensive Curly told Gabe and Barney. "This here one's a mossy horn. He's in his prime. I venture to say he's got five, six hundred pounds on that youngster I just clipped."

This time it was Gabe's loop which descended on the steer's neck and was pulled tight. The animal fought to free himself of Gabe's rope but could barely move its head.

Curly yelled, "Give him a little slack, Gabe, so Barney can make a heel catch."

Gabe did so, and the steer, the instant the rope went slack, turned and tried to run. The movement was just enough to allow Barney, who was circling around Gabe, Curly, and the steer, to catch its heels in a narrow loop which he promptly pulled tight.

Working in concert with Barney, Gabe reeled in his rope until there was no slack left in it. The steer continued to struggle but to no avail. Like the one before it, it went down with a thud and lay on the ground loudly bawling its futile protests.

Curly bounded up to the animal, saw in hand, and propped one knee against the steer's neck. He began to saw, holding tightly to the horn he was attempting to sever. The steer tried to fight him off by turning its head from side to side, but because its horns were so long, they kept striking the ground before they could do any damage.

Curly sawed on, white fragments of bone flying as he worked.

Gabe dismounted. Leaving his buckskin in position to hold the steer in place, he went over to the fire and removed the iron Curly had replaced after using it on the first steer. He carried it back to where Curly was still vigorously sawing and flecks of blood were staining the mossy growth at the base of the steer's horns. He stood there with the iron in his hand and waited. He didn't have to wait long.

Curly's saw bit through the thick horn which fell to the ground amid a shower of bright red blood. Gabe stepped up to the animal and thrust the glowing end of the iron against the bleeding horn to cauterize it. The steer screamed as smoke rose from its wound and the blood in it sizzled.

"Nasty damned business," Curly muttered through clenched teeth as he began to saw through the steer's remaining horn. Ten minutes later, it was all over. The second horn lay on the ground not far from the first.

Tendrils of smoke rose from the second wound Gabe had just cauterized.

After returning the iron to the fire, Gabe called out, "Ready, Barney?"

When the other drover nodded, Gabe advised, "Step lively, Curly. We're about to let loose that thousand pounds of live dynamite lying down there."

Curly turned and ran.

Gabe shook out his loop which came off the steer's neck at the same time that Barney freed his rope and began to reel it in.

The steer stumbled to its feet and went racing away to rejoin the herd.

"There's the next likely candidate," Gabe said, pointing to another mossy horn standing motionless on the edge of the herd which had been paying no attention to the previous proceedings. "His horns are twisted all out of shape. They're bound to do damage to himself or any animal or man that gets too close to him. You want to rope him first, Barney?"

Barney never got to answer the question because at that instant Dillworth, who had been patrolling the cattle's bed ground on horseback, shouted, "All hands and the cook!"

The traditional cry that summoned the men working a drive when trouble—a stampede, a fire—had started rallied all the drovers at once.

Gabe quickly coiled his rope and hung it on his saddle horn. He went galloping toward the spot where Dillworth was stiffly sitting his saddle, his gun now in his hand. Barney rode beside Gabe, and Curly brought up the rear, running as fast as his feet would carry him.

None of the three had to ask why they had been summoned. The answer to that question was perfectly apparent. In the distance, Jackson Wolf with three other Lighthorsemen, but minus William Colbert, the stock superintendent, were riding at a fast clip toward the cow camp.

CHAPTER SIX

"Get ready," Dillworth told Gabe, Barney, and Curly as they rode up to join him and the rest of the drovers. "Do whatever you have to to protect the herd."

There was silence then as Gabe and the others watched the Lighthorsemen approach. Jackson Wolf's expression was unreadable. The men with him rode easy and looked as if they might merely be out for an afternoon canter. But the eyes of all four men were steely and their jaws were set.

"I've brought the permit," Wolf announced as he and his men drew rein about fifteen yards away from Dillworth and his drovers. When Dillworth did not acknowledge the remark by either word or deed, Wolf continued. "I trust you are ready to sign it and pay the twenty-five dollars and other fees we discussed yesterday."

Still Dillworth said nothing.

"There's another matter we've come about this morning," Wolf declared, his gaze shifting back and forth among the assembled drovers.

"What other matter?" Dillworth asked suspiciously, testily.

"Which one of your men is named Dave?"

Dillworth frowned. "Are you referring to Dave Carmody?"

"I don't know the man's last name. Only the first. I have been given a rough physical description of him. Based on that description, I don't believe I see him among your drovers. Or am I mistaken about that?"

"You're not mistaken. Carmody's not here."

"Where is he?"

"What the hell business is that of yours?" Dillworth snapped.

Wolf, unruffled by the trail boss' outburst, repeated, "Where is he, do you know?"

"I don't know."

"Are you hiding him?"

"Why the hell would I be hiding him?" an incredulous Dillworth spluttered.

"Because of what he's done."

"Look, Wolf, the last time I saw Dave Carmody was last night before he went to town. He hasn't come back." Dillworth turned to the men on his right. "Any of you seen him?" When he received a negative answer, he consulted the drovers on his left and received the same kind of response. No one had seen Dave Carmody since the night before.

"If it's Carmody you want," Dillworth told Wolf, "you'd best ride on out of here and start looking for him elsewhere because he's not in camp."

Wolf turned and said something in the Chickasaw language to the mounted man next to him.

"Where does he think he's going?" Dillworth asked as the Lighthorseman rode away.

Wolf didn't answer the question. He watched his man approach the chuck wagon, stand up in his stirrups, and root about among the soogans, tarps, and bedrolls piled haphazardly in the wagon's bed. Moments later, he rode back to rejoin Wolf and the others.

"There's nobody hiding in that wagon," he told Wolf.

"I could have told you that," Dillworth said. "Now, do you mind telling me just what the Sam Hill this is all about?"

Wolf's right hand dropped toward the butt of his gun.

The drover named Barney drew his gun swiftly and fired a single shot which barely missed Wolf.

One of the Lighthorsemen with Wolf promptly returned fire, nicking Barney in the arm.

Drovers and Lighthorsemen alike ran for cover wherever they could find it. Gabe dismounted and, keeping behind his horse, ran it toward the chuck wagon. He circled the wagon and crouched down behind it. He had no sooner done so than a shot rang out and hit the lantern sitting atop the chuck box, shattering it. The shot, Gabe was dismayed to realize, had come from Curly who was crouching behind a pile of supplies not far away. The drover had taken aim at one of the Lighthorsemen but had almost hit Gabe.

As the Chickasaws dropped down out of sight—one behind a hummock, Wolf behind some of the cattle, and the other two policemen behind the trunks of trees, Gabe cocked his revolver. He didn't want to shoot, but he also didn't want to be shot. He felt he had no choice but to draw his gun, and he also knew that he had better be willing to fire it in self-defense if that became necessary and never mind the ins and outs of this particular dispute. Never mind who was right and who was wrong. Forget trying to reach a compromise. It seemed to him that the time for compromise was past—at least for now.

When the shooting stopped, maybe some calm talk could settle the problem. Or if Carmody were to show up—that might calm things down. Gabe wondered what Carmody might have done to warrant arrest by the Lighthorsemen. His wondering was cut short by a round that tore into the water barrel strapped to the chuck wagon. The sound of water pouring out of the barrel reached his ears although he was on the opposite side of the wagon from the barrel.

Shots continued to be exchanged but, as far as Gabe could tell, no one had been hit other than the drover named Barney who had started the fracas. No, he corrected himself, that wasn't quite right. It was Jackson Wolf's going for his gun that had actually started the shoot-out.

The Chickasaw's action puzzled Gabe. Wolf seemed like a steady sort, not the type to fly off the handle. But Gabe himself had seen him go for his gun.

Gabe scanned the area while keeping low in order not to make a target of himself. He couldn't see Wolf at first, but then the man showed himself from where he was now hunkered down behind a pile of frost-cracked boulders. Behind Wolf was a thick stand of timber. As Gabe watched, Wolf sprang to his feet and made a beeline for the shelter of the trees. He almost didn't make it. One of the drovers, spotting the Lighthorsemen leader's tactic, suddenly straightened up. With both hands gripping his revolver, he took aim at the racing Wolf.

Gabe also rose. He took aim and shot the gun out of the startled drover's hands.

"Jesus crucified Christ!" Dillworth roared from his cover behind a cluster of bawling cows. "What the hell are you doing shooting at somebody on your own side, Conrad?"

Gabe didn't bother to answer the question. He didn't try to explain that he had shot the gun out of the drover's hand to keep the man from killing Wolf. If he had explained that much, yelling at the top of his lungs over the continuing sound of gunfire, he would have had to go on to explain that he had done so to keep the drover from doing something he might have cause later to regret.

He could hear Dillworth cursing in the distance. As Gabe held his fire and watched with growing unease the scene unfolding in front of him, the wounded Barney got together with two of his companions at one end of the chuck wagon and conferred briefly.

Gabe was close enough to them to overhear a few words of their heated conversation.

"—charge them," from Barney.

"—mow 'em all down," from one of the other drovers.

"—go get 'em," from the third man of the trio.

"Hold it!" Gabe called out to them in an effort to stop what he considered their ill-advised plan. Perhaps they didn't hear him. In any event, the three men burst out into the open, their six-guns spitting fire, and went zigzagging across the open expanse of ground that separated them from their Chickasaw enemies.

Lighthorsemen's rounds kicked up dust in front of and on both sides of the three men who had launched their frontal attack which Gabe considered nothing more than utter folly. He squeezed off a round in the direction of the Indians, aiming deliberately high in order not to hit anyone. He felt he had to do something to try to protect the drovers, even if he thought they were acting foolishly. They were offering themselves as perfect targets, probably out of some misguided notion of bravery. He fired a quick volley of shots over the heads of the three drovers advancing on the Lighthorsemen's position.

He couldn't help smiling to himself when his shots caused Barney and his two companions to drop to the ground and take cover behind a stand of bramble bushes. They must have thought the rounds came from the Chickasaws, he reasoned. Maybe now they'll stay put and out of harm's way.

Maybe. But even if they did stay where they were, they still might be killed. For what? For nothing, that's what. With that bitter thought uppermost in his mind, Gabe knew what he was going to do. He leaped over the rump of his buckskin and once in the saddle headed for the woods. He had not gone far when a shot screamed over his head. A shot Jackson Wolf had fired at him from the cover of the trees.

He veered to the left and guided his horse in among the trees. Once there, he slid out of the saddle and quickly kicked the remains of a deadfall he found into a makeshift breastwork. Bellying down behind it, he propped the barrel of his gun on the rotting wood and scanned the shaded area. He saw a squirrel pretending by means of immobility not to be where it was. He saw a column of ants marching across the forest floor. He did not see Jackson Wolf.

But he learned where the Chickasaw was when a second shot came whining his way. The flash of fire from the muzzle of Wolf's gun revealed the man's whereabouts. Over to the right. About thirty yards away. Down on one knee behind the trunk of a loblolly pine.

Gabe took aim at a branch directly above Wolf's position and fired. The branch broke and fell to the ground. Wolf's body lurched as he sought a more secure position. Gabe, as he thumbed fresh shells out of his cartridge belt and into the empty chambers of his revolver, smiled and took aim again. This time his shot skinned bark off the tree Wolf was hiding behind.

Wolf's head and gun hand suddenly appeared. The Lighthorseman sent a snap shot in Gabe's direction and then ducked back behind the tree's trunk. Gabe returned fire, sending more tree bark whirling up into the air.

Almost before the bark had struck the ground, he was racing through the woods, running the way he had been taught by the Oglala Sioux when he was but a boy, making only the smallest of sounds. He circled around Wolf's position and in a matter of just a few minutes he was hunkered down behind some rocks and taking potentially deadly aim at Wolf's back. He watched Wolf fire at the deadfall and then push his hat back on his head and wait. When there was no return fire from behind the deadfall, Wolf eased out from behind his tree and peered into the shadows lurking beneath the trees.

Wolf raised his gun.

Gabe took another step in his direction.

Wolf fired and then quickly took cover again.

Gabe moved closer to him, his gun raised.

Wolf was reloading his revolver when the barrel of Gabe's gun bored into the small of his back.

Wolf stiffened, started to turn his head, but then raised his hands instead. He said, "I hope you're not a back-shooter."

"Never was. Never will be."

Gabe heard the faint sigh of breath ease past Wolf's lips.

"What now?" the Lighthorseman asked.

"Drop your gun, and we'll go back to where all this started and see if we can't work things out."

"The law's the law," Wolf said and dropped his gun.

"I'm not arguing that point," Gabe said as he retrieved the weapon.

"You men won't obey it."

"I'm willing to obey it. It's not me you have to herd into line. It's Mr. Dillworth."

"What's your name?"

"Gabe Conrad."

"I'm happy you're not a back-shooter, Gabe Conrad."

"March, mister."

Wolf marched, his hands still in the air, through and then out of the woods. He halted abruptly at the continuing sound of gunfire coming from the cow camp and the sight of his men fleeing on their horses. He swore.

"Looks like round two's over," Gabe said. "You can put your hands down now. Only don't try anything foolish like you did back there in the cow camp when you went for your gun."

"When I went for my—I didn't go for my gun back there. I was reaching for a warrant I had in my pocket. A warrant for the arrest of Dave Carmody." Wolf slowly turned to face Gabe. "You're the man who urged Dillworth to obey Chickasaw law during our confrontation yesterday."

"I'm the one."

"You surprised me. I thought all you drovers were hell-bent on having things your way."

"You might as well be on your way, Wolf, since the gunfight seems to be over. Unless you want to take on Dillworth and the rest of his men by your lonesome."

"I have no wish to do that."

Gabe holstered his gun, handed Wolf's over, and started walking toward the spot where his buckskin was browsing the brush.

"Wait."

He turned to face Wolf, noting with hidden relief that the Indian had leathered his revolver.

"I was thinking that maybe you would like to come with me and hear what happened—what your friend, Carmody, did last night. Maybe after you hear the Chickasaw side of the story, you might consider siding with me and my men the next time we go up against Dillworth and his drovers."

Gabe was about to reject the suggestion. But there was something about it that intrigued him. Not just the fact that if he went along with it, he'd find out what Carmody had done—was alleged by this Lighthorseman to have done—but also what kind of a man Jackson Wolf was and why he was making an overture to him when he had to consider Gabe one of the enemy.

"You might, once you hear what the involved woman, Annie Sadler, has to say," Wolf continued, "see things our way and be willing to help us present our case against Dave Carmody to your trail boss."

Annie Sadler. Gabe remembered the woman at the log cabin. He had drunk from her well while hunting strayed steers. The mention of her name decided him. If Annie Sadler was somehow involved with Dave Carmody, he wanted to hear about it. Was that the truth? Or did he simply want the chance to see, to be near, the lovely Annie Sadler once more? He thrust those questions aside, refusing to try to answer them.

"Get your horse, Wolf, and let's go," he said.

They drew rein in front of the Sadler cabin and dismounted. They were wrapping their reins around the hitch rail in front of the building when the door was opened by the elderly man Gabe had seen driving the carriage the other day.

"Is this the one?" he asked, pointing a bony finger at Gabe.

"This man's name is Gabe Conrad," Jackson Wolf said. To Gabe, he said, "This is Harley Sadler. He's Annie's grandfather."

"How do, Mr. Sadler?" Gabe said.

"Is this the one?" Sadler repeated, ignoring Gabe's outstretched hand.

"No, he's not," Wolf answered. "But he's with the drive that's camped at the Washita. The one that the man named Dave—Dave Carmody—is associated with."

"Then what did you bring him here for if he's not the one?" Sadler asked. "Where's the one that did it—the one named Dave? Dave Carmody, did you say?" Sadler turned bleary eyes on Wolf.

"He wasn't at the cow camp when I got there. So I couldn't bring him. I brought Conrad so he could hear Annie's side of the story."

"What good's that gonna do anybody, tell me that?" Sadler snapped.

"It might convince Conrad to side with us in the matter."

"But he's white. What made you think—" Sadler almost collapsed in a fit of coughing and ragged wheezing. When it finally ended, he wiped his wet lips and muttered, "I smoke too much." He took out a cigar and lit it. "But they give these short sixes away free in the saloon, so I find it hard to refuse them."

Gabe waved away the cloud of smoke Sadler blew in his direction and said, "You were wondering if a white man would find it possible to come down on the Indian side of a dispute with white men, is that it, Mr. Sadler?"

"You're damn right, that's it."

Gabe stepped to one side to avoid the foul-smelling smoke from Sadler's stogie. "I consider myself a fair man," he said. "I'd like to hear what happened to your granddaughter. Maybe I can play a hand in helping to right whatever's wrong."

"The only way the wrong done to my girl is going to be righted is to tie up that Dave what's-his-name and lay a bullwhip on his bare back."

Gabe glanced at Wolf who explained, "The traditional Chickasaw punishment for a man who rapes a woman is twenty lashes."

"Do I understand you to say that Dave Carmody raped Annie Sadler?" Gabe inquired, frowning.

"That's what Annie claims," Wolf replied.

Sadler coughed and then spat. "What do you mean 'claims', Jackson? Don't you believe the girl?"

"I believe her. It was just a manner of speaking, Mr. Sadler. I didn't mean to cast doubt on Annie's version of what happened."

"I'd like to hear what she has to say," Gabe said.

Sadler beckoned and then turned and reentered the cabin.

Gabe and Wolf followed him inside.

"Annie, girl, come on out here," he called out. "We got guests. They want to have a word with you."

When Annie neither appeared nor offered a response to her grandfather's summons, Sadler yelled, "Don't you start with that shy-as-a-shrinking-violet act again with me, girl!" He strode across the puncheon floor and flung open a door on the far side of the room. He disappeared for a moment and, when he reappeared, he had a firm, one-handed grip on both of his granddaughter's wrists and was practically dragging her into the room.

"Hello, Annie," Gabe said. "It's nice to see you again."

Annie kept her face turned away from him and Wolf as she struggled but failed to free herself.

"Sit you down there at the table, girl," Sadler ordered. He shoved his granddaughter into a chair and stood over her. "Now tell this stranger what happened last night."

Annie shook her head as she kept her eyes averted.

But Gabe saw the two tears that rolled silently down her cheeks.

Wolf went to her and gently placed a hand on her shoulder.

She flinched as he did so.

"Maybe if Annie doesn't want to talk to me," Gabe said, "it'd be best if I moved on."

"Annie, this man's name is—" Wolf began.

"I know who he is." Annie's voice was almost inaudible. "He came by here wanting water for himself and his horse."

"I'm still grateful to you for letting me have some," Gabe said.

"He wants to help if he can," Wolf told Annie. "To do that, he's got to know what happened. He's got to know what that man did to you."

"Dave," Annie murmured. "He said his name was Dave. He was so nice to me at first. I never thought . . ."

Gabe and Wolf exchanged glances as Annie's words trailed away.

"She was out late at night," Sadler said, his voice close

to a snarl. "She should have been in bed where she belonged at that hour, not prowling around outside in the dark."

Annie stiffened. She turned her head sharply to stare at Sadler. Fire flashed in her eyes. Gone was the stricken tearful girl. In her place now was a strong, determined woman.

"Grandpapa, I did nothing wrong!"

Her words had been clearly and firmly spoken.

Sadler responded with, "Had you brought yourself to bed at a halfway decent hour what happened wouldn't have."

"Why are you blaming me, Grandpapa?" she asked, the sound of injured innocence in her tone. She turned to Gabe. "I had served supper and had finished washing the dishes. I carried the dishpan outside and dumped the water. I was about to go back inside when the moon came out from some clouds." She looked up as if she could see the moon now through the ceiling rafters. "It was so beautiful. The night was warm. There were fireflies about." She smiled at the memory. "Like little orange harvest moons, they were here, there, and everywhere. They seemed determined not to be outdone by the moon riding up there so high in the sky."

"Get on with it, girl!" Sadler urged.

"Let her tell it in her own way and in her own good time," Wolf said sharply. His tone silenced Sadler who slumped grumbling into a chair and sat there puffing on his short six.

"Go ahead, Annie," Wolf urged in a low tone of voice. "You saw the moon. The fireflies."

"Yes. It was a truly lovely night. I put down the dishpan and climbed the hummock on the side of the house. When I got to the top, I threw myself down on the ground on my back and just lay there staring up at the sky—at the moon. It seemed—for a minute it seemed—as if there was no one else in the world. Only me and the moon.

"I could smell the grass and the sweet clover. There was a breeze blowing, a warm breeze. I closed my eyes and imagined—oh, all sorts of things."

Annie slowly rose from her chair and walked to the window. She drew aside the muslin curtain covering it and stared out into the night that had fallen since Gabe and Wolf arrived at the cabin.

"I heard hoofbeats. A prince passing by, I told myself. A prince with wildflowers in his hair on his way home to his kingdom where his princess was waiting for him. The sound of his hoofbeats faded away and then were gone. Time passed. I don't know how long it was before I opened my eyes . . ."

Annie let the curtain fall back into place. With her back still turned to the three men in the room, all of whom were watching her intently, she lowered her head. When her voice came again, it was unsteady, tremulous.

"He was standing there looking down at me."

When she said nothing more for a long moment, Wolf prompted, "Dave Carmody."

Annie nodded once. " 'Nice night, ain't it?' was what he said to me.

"I sat up and smoothed my dress. 'Yes,' I said. 'It is a nice night.'

" 'I was passing by,' he said, 'and saw you here. Thought I'd stop and say howdy.'

" 'I have to go inside now,' I told him. But when I started down the hill, he caught up with me. He didn't touch me—not then, he didn't. But he stepped in front of me and blocked my way. I tried to step around him, but he moved in front of me again.

" 'The night's young,' he said. I remember him saying that. 'The night's young.' "

Annie returned to her chair and sat down. She folded her hands in her lap and looked down at them. " 'My name's Dave,' he said. 'What's yours?'

" 'Annie,' I answered. 'I live in that cabin yonder with my Grandpa. He's waiting on me.'

"I tried again to get around him, but he caught me up in his arms and before I knew what was happening, he was kissing me. It was—awful."

Annie grimaced. Her hand rose and wiped her lips as she gazed unseeing into a corner of the room.

"He kissed you," Wolf said softly.

"Yes. Then—then he—his hand—he held me so tight with one hand pressing against my back that I couldn't move, and his other hand—it was his right hand—it—he put it on my bosom. He squeezed me there and kept kissing me. My lips. My neck.

"I tried to push him away, but I couldn't." Annie's head snapped up, and she stared at Gabe, her eyes haunted. "I *did* try to push him away. I tried *hard* to!"

Gabe nodded.

"Then?" Wolf prompted in his soft voice.

"He pushed me down to the ground. He held me there. I couldn't move. You see, he was covering me. His hands were under my dress. I remember the night suddenly felt cold when he tore my dress and my body was exposed to the breeze. I tried to scream. I tried to call out to Grandpapa to come help me, but he put a hand over my mouth and I couldn't. Then—he had his way with me."

Annie sobbed once, choking back the sound with the back of one fisted hand.

Sadler stubbed out his cigar and muttered an oath. He glanced at Wolf. "What are you going to do now? Let that rapist get away with what he did?"

"He's not going to get away with it," Wolf assured the old man.

Sadler snorted and rose. He went to a wall cupboard, opened it, and took down a bottle of whiskey. He uncorked it with his teeth and drank from it. Lowering the bottle, he licked his lips and said, "If I were a younger man, I'd go out after him my own self. And when I found him, I'd kill the bastard with my own two hands."

As Sadler took another drink, a deep one this time, Annie looked up and said, "It makes no difference whether or not you arrest him. What's done is done, and it can't be undone."

"He's got to pay!" Sadler cried, waving the bottle about. "He can't be allowed to get away with what he did. That man, why, he's one of the *Lofas* incarnate."

Gabe glanced at Wolf who explained, "Lofas, we Chickasaws believe, are supernatural beings who are the scourge of our people. They hide game from our hunters, carry off women, cause all kinds of personal disasters, both large and small."

"A Lofa, that's what he is," Sadler intoned and took another drink. He glared at Wolf. "Are you afraid of Lofas?"

"No, I am not."

"Then why stand you here like this, talking and doing nothing to this Lofa—this Dave Carmody, as he calls himself? Why are you not out searching for him so that he may be brought to justice? Chickasaw justice? Our law demands—"

"I know the law," Wolf interrupted.

"Twenty lashes!" Sadler blurted out.

"Annie," Gabe said, "I'd like to ask you a question."

She looked at him uneasily. "I've told you what happened."

"What did this fellow who said his name was Dave look like?"

"You think she has named the wrong man?" Wolf asked sharply.

Gabe ignored him. "Annie?"

"It was dark," she said. "But the moon was bright. I saw him clearly." She gave a description of the man who had attacked her which left not the slightest doubt in Gabe's mind that the man was indeed Dave Carmody.

"Let's ride on back to the cow camp," Gabe suggested to Wolf. "Maybe Carmody's showed up there by now."

"Just the two of us?"

"We could sneak up on the camp. Get a drop on them. Make them turn Carmody over to you—if he's there."

"They'd shoot me as quick as look at me."

"Not if we get the drop on them like I reckon we can do if we work together."

"It's a risky business. You sure you want to try it?"

"I'm sure."

"Why?" Annie suddenly asked, gazing intently at Gabe.

"Why?" He shrugged his shoulders. "Maybe because I once met a lady who was kind enough to let me draw water from her well when I was thirsty."

Their eyes met and held.

"Let's go," Wolf said.

"Bring that Lofa back here," Sadler called after them as Gabe and Wolf made their way out of the cabin. "I want to be the one to whip the life out of him!"

"It's a shame this had to happen to Annie Sadler," Wolf said as he rode beside Gabe on the way to the cow camp. "She's not had a good life since her parents died and she went to live with her grandfather."

"Sadler struck me as a rough old fellow. I couldn't for the life of me understand why he'd go and blame Annie for the rape."

"Sadler probably feels guilty about not having prevented it. So he blames Annie to weasel his way out of his sense of guilt. He was probably drunk the night it happened to top things off, although I shouldn't say that since I can't prove it."

"He likes the bottle, does he?"

"More than a little bit. When he came running up to my cabin last night to report the rape, he was slurring his speech and wasn't all that steady on his feet. It's too bad about the old man. He used to be our Principal Chief, but then he started to drink pretty heavily. I guess things caught up with him at long last."

"Things?"

"He lost his parents on the Trail of Tears. They both froze to death. His wife went crazy during the trip; she couldn't stand the strain. She's in an asylum up in Ardmore, and they say there's not much of a chance that she'll ever be sane enough to be let out again. Chief Sadler was a fighter in his day, but I guess there comes a time when the fight goes out of a man. There comes a day when he just can't bear the burden of pain he's been toting around for so long. He's just got to give in and lay it down. When that day comes, it's like a little death. That's what happened to Sadler. The drink gradually got a good strong grip on him, and he couldn't shake himself free of it no matter how hard he tried to. I've seen him more than once or twice in the saloon up in the pines behind his house cadging drinks off anyone who would listen to his tale of woe."

"Why doesn't Annie strike out on her own? Make a life for herself without the old man?"

"I think she just can't bring herself to leave him. She feels sorry for him. Wants to help him."

"Can she? Under the circumstances?"

Wolf sighed. "I doubt it. But she tries. She puts up with his abuse and then dries his tears when he goes on a crying jag and asks her to forgive him because he's not the man he used to be. Without Annie, Sadler would be lost."

"There's light up ahead," Gabe said. "Must be the cow camp's fire. Draw rein, and we'll go forward from here on foot."

Both men dismounted and fastened the reins of their horses to branches of a chokecherry bush. Wolf drew his gun as they moved through the dark night toward the faint glow of the camp's cook fire in the distance.

On the way, Gabe reached out and touched Wolf's shoulder. When he had the Lighthorseman's attention, he pointed to the woods that Wolf had hidden in earlier. They made their way there, bending over and keeping low in order not to be seen.

Once within the shelter of the trees, they moved forward more swiftly until they reached the edge of the woods.

The scene before them was placid enough—or appeared to be. Drovers sat around the campfire drinking coffee and talking in low tones. Two night riders were circling the herd some distance away. Dillworth was seated on a cracker barrel next to the chuck wagon. Several men were sleeping on the ground wrapped up in their soogans.

A seemingly placid scene.

But Gabe noticed that the sleeping men had placed their guns on the ground by their sides. The flap on Dillworth's holster was raised and tucked under the trail boss' belt. The two night riders were silent as they made their rounds instead of singing softly to the cattle as was the custom of most men while on night guard.

"We'll take one of the night guards," Gabe whispered to

Wolf. "When they've passed one another and are circling the herd in opposite directions—then we'll make our move. Follow me."

Wolf followed Gabe as he moved to the left and began to weave his way through the trees toward the herd's bed ground in the distance.

Gabe moved as silently as a shadow through the woods as he headed for the night rider circling the herd up ahead of him. Beside him Wolf moved just as swiftly and silently. Both men seemed able to read the other's thoughts, so perfectly did their movements synchronize.

Gabe slowed, came to a halt, and held up a hand. Wolf also halted and stared at the man Gabe had pointed out who was riding slowly through the darkness toward them. When Gabe pointed again, Wolf moved to the right. Then Gabe and the Lighthorseman waited as the rider came closer. Moments later, as Curly rode into a pool of moonlight, Gabe, his gun drawn, stepped into the white light and said, "Step down and cool your saddle, Curly."

Curly went for his gun.

Wolf, coming at him from the opposite side, seized and twisted his wrist, causing his gun to fall to the ground. The Lighthorseman pulled Curly out of the saddle and placed his free hand over the startled man's mouth to keep him from giving away their presence.

Gabe stepped up close to the wide-eyed Curly who was staring at him as if he were a demon who had just materialized in an otherwise safe night.

"Don't call out," Gabe ordered. "Don't make a sound. We're not here to hurt you. We're here to do a little old-fashioned bargaining. You, as it happens, are our high card."

Curly managed to shake his head from side to side.

A denial? Of what? Gabe wondered.

"Wolf'll take his hand from your mouth if you'll not let out a yell when he does. Will you promise to keep quiet, Curly?"

Curly managed a nod.

Wolf, at a signal from Gabe, took his hand away from

the drover's mouth but stood ready to clap it back in place if Curly tried to give the alarm.

"What is this, Gabe?" Curly asked. "What are you doing here with *him*?"

"Him and me are partners for the time being. We came to talk turkey with Mr. Dillworth, but since there's only the two of us, we figured we'd better have something to bargain with. Like I said before, you're that something."

"I don't get it."

"We plan to tell Mr. Dillworth that we'll shoot you if he doesn't meet our demands."

Fear flared in Curly's eyes. "You'd shoot me, Gabe?"

"Let's head for the camp," Gabe said.

The muzzle of Wolf's gun rammed into Curly's back.

"I'm on my way," the drover said. "Don't shoot me!"

Curly moved out, leaving his horse behind. Minutes later, when the three men walked into the light of the camp's cook fire, Dillworth shot to his feet.

"What the hell?"

"Take it easy," Gabe told him. "The rest of you fellows, if any of you takes a notion to make a wrong move, I'll let light through your friend Curly here. Is that understood?"

There were rumblings of protest, but none of the men in the camp went for their guns. The sleepers awoke and sat up blinking in the firelight at Gabe, Wolf, and Curly.

"What do you want?" Dillworth asked stiffly, his right hand suspended in midair about eight inches away from the revolver holstered on his hip.

"Dave Carmody," Wolf answered.

"That's what this is all about?"

"That's right, Mr. Dillworth," Gabe said. "Where is he?"

Dillworth began to laugh. He threw his head back and shook with merriment.

Gabe and Wolf exchanged puzzled glances.

Dillworth stopped laughing. "Carmody's not here."

"You're lying," Wolf said sharply.

"No, he's not," Curly said in a frightened voice. "Gabe, Mr. Dillworth's telling you the truth. Carmody did come

back here right after the shoot-out, but Mr. Dillworth told
him—"

"I told him," Dillworth interrupted, "that some Chickasaw
savages had come by here looking for him. I told him that
we ran the heathens off like the pack of cowardly curs they
were."

Wolf glared at Dillworth, anger in his eyes.

"Where's Carmody now?" Gabe asked as the drovers
scattered around the fire stared in a strained and sullen
silence at him.

As Dillworth started to answer the question, he was
silenced by the sound of a shot that tore through the air,
narrowly missing Jackson Wolf.

CHAPTER SEVEN

"Take cover!" Gabe yelled as he seized Curly and dragged him around behind the chuck wagon.

At the same time, Wolf threw himself to the ground, rolled over, and came up behind the cracker barrel Dillworth had been sitting on.

Both men scanned the area, searching for the source of the shot that had almost hit the Lighthorseman. They found it when a second shot whined through the air toward them.

Gabe squeezed off a round, aiming for the spot in the darkness from which the muzzle flash had come.

"Owww!"

"You got him!" Wolf exulted and fired at the spot where the cry of pain had just come from.

Gabe dragged Curly out from behind the chuck wagon into the open. "Throw your gun down, or this drover dies!" he called out to the unseen gunman. "Come in with your hands high!"

"Do it!" Curly cried as he trembled in Gabe's firm grip. "You don't, and I'm a dead man. Please!" he pleaded.

A tense moment passed during which none of the drovers spoke or moved. Dillworth stood rigid, his hand on the butt of his gun. But he did not draw it.

"Don't shoot!"

The resonant voice had come barreling out of the darkness. It was followed a moment later by the appearance of a man Gabe immediately recognized as one of Dillworth's drovers.

"I threw my gun down back there like you said," the man told Gabe as blood from a flesh wound ran down his bare forearm. He halted, and his eyes flicked to Dillworth the trail boss.

"Mr. Dillworth, sir," he said, "I figured there was something amiss when Curly didn't meet me while I was circling the herd. I came here looking for him and saw those two"— he indicated Gabe and Wolf—"holding you all under their guns. So I tried to put them out of action."

Gabe gestured peremptorily with his revolver, and the night rider went to stand beside Dillworth.

"Now that things have settled down again," Gabe began, "let's get back to the subject at hand. Namely, where's Carmody?"

"In Ardmore," Dillworth muttered. "I sent him up there to send telegraph messages to the owners of these cattle we're driving. I wanted to know if they'd be willing to put up the money to pay what the Indian son of a bitch over there is demanding for his permit and precious goddamn grass."

Dillworth's eyes narrowed. "Do I get to ask a question or is this strictly a one-sided show?"

"Ask away," Gabe replied.

"What does that Indian want Carmody for?"

"This Indian," Wolf snapped, "wants your drover for raping the woman who drove by your herd the day before yesterday with her grandfather. And I'm going to get him sooner or later."

"The last I heard the law in the Nations was enforced by marshals who ride for Judge Parker out of Fort Smith, Arkansas."

"We Lighthorsemen also have jurisdiction in the Nations," Wolf pointed out. "We work together with the marshals— when they're around. They're not at the moment. So it's up to me and my men to handle matters like the rape of a Chickasaw woman by your drover."

"How do you know Dave raped her?" Dillworth shot at Wolf. "From all I've heard, your Indian females aren't exactly models of virtue and chastity any more than bitches in heat are."

"Mr. Dillworth, you've got a foul mouth, did anybody ever tell you that?" Wolf said evenly. "You've also got a swamp where your mind ought to be."

"Proof," Dillworth said, his tone making the word a taunt.

"I've got proof," Wolf declared. "The woman who was raped will identify Carmody in a Chickasaw trial."

Dillworth snorted contemptuously. "You call that proof? An Indian whore's word against that of a white man?"

"The woman in question would have no reason to point the finger at Carmody unless he did the deed," Gabe interjected.

"Is that so?" Dillworth planted his hands on his hips as he confronted Gabe. "Maybe this woman's been diddling some Chickasaw buck, and now that she finds herself pregnant, she's made up her wily mind to point an accusing finger in some other direction than the one where it should be pointed."

"The woman in question doesn't even know Carmody," Gabe pointed out. "At least, she didn't until he attacked her near her home."

"Wait a minute," Dillworth said thoughtfully. "Wait just one minute here. You're claiming she didn't know Carmody, am I right?"

"That's right," Gabe said. "She gave Wolf a description of the man who raped her and that description fit Carmody like a glove."

Dillworth began to smile. "I'm sure it did."

Gabe wondered why Dillworth was smiling like a cat lapping cream and acting so confident.

"Wolf, you said before that the woman you claim Carmody raped drove by the herd the other day with her grandfather, as I recollect."

The Lighthorseman nodded.

"She saw Carmody," Dillworth said, "when she drove

by. Later, when she decided to put on her little act to
account for her pregnancy, she pointed the finger at a man
she remembered having seen with the herd. A man named
Dave Carmody."

Jackson Wolf looked suddenly crestfallen.

He did, that is, until Gabe spoke up. "That theory of
yours, Dillworth, as neat as it sounds, doesn't hold up. Ask
yourself this. How'd she know Carmody's first name which
she gave to Wolf?"

"Whose side are you on, Conrad? Your own kind or these
savages?"

"I'm on Wolf's side in this particular matter."

"Why you Indian-loving bastard!" Dillworth sprang forward and kicked the gun out of Gabe's hand. He swung
and landed a roundhouse right, causing Gabe to lose his
hold on Curly.

Gabe quickly recovered from the trail boss' blow. He
retaliated with a left uppercut that snapped Dillworth's head
backward.

"Don't anybody move!" Wolf shouted, seizing Curly by
the nape of the neck in one hand and brandishing the gun
he held in the other.

The drovers remained in position as Dillworth kicked
Gabe in the shin and Gabe smashed a fist into the side of
the man's face, breaking the skin and bringing blood which
began to seep down Dillworth's cheek.

Dillworth struck out with his right fist, but the blow
glanced harmlessly off Gabe's shoulder.

"Kill the Indian-loving son of a bitch, Boss!" the drover
named Barney yelled.

Gabe delivered a gut punch that knocked the wind out of
Dillworth. The trail boss seized his stomach in both hands
and took a step backward, his cheeks filling with sucked-in
air. Then, his eyes blazing, he lunged at Gabe. He rammed
a fist into Gabe's stomach, but it did not damage the mass
of solid muscle it encountered there.

Gabe chopped down with his right fist, hitting Dillworth
on the left shoulder. The man's knees buckled, and he
almost went down.

But he managed to remain standing. He moved in on Gabe, feinting first and then delivering a savage series of blows that sent Gabe staggering backward. He kicked out and caught Gabe in the shin again. He jabbed with his left and then with his right. His right connected with Gabe's jaw.

He raised his booted foot, ready to kick again. But Gabe seized the boot in both hands and twisted it. Dillworth let out a yell, lost his balance, and fell to the ground.

Gabe stepped back to get his breath and to let the pain in his shin and jaw subside. Dillworth scrambled to his feet and lunged at Gabe for the knockout punch, but Gabe swiftly retreated. As Dillworth pursued him, Gabe, sidestepped and then swung both fists.

One caught the trail boss on the forehead with the force of a sledgehammer, forcing him backward. Gabe moved forward and let go with a fast flurry of telling blows to his opponent's body which brought a series of grunts and then a drawn-out groan from Dillworth. The trail boss suddenly doubled over and, waving both arms to knock Gabe's raised fists aside, he slammed his head into Gabe's chest, knocking him down. Before Gabe could recover from the unexpected attack, Dillworth kicked him in the ribs.

Pain shot through Gabe's torso. He rolled out of the way of Dillworth's flying boot and got to his feet. Knocking the trail boss' fists aside, he landed a savage blow on Dillworth's chin. He sidestepped a retaliatory blow, feinted with his left, and slammed a hard right under Dillworth's guard which smashed into the right side of the man's jaw.

Seemingly unfazed by the blow, Dillworth moved in and clinched with Gabe. As they struggled, Gabe managed to break free of the man's grip. He danced to the left, feinted, and ducked a Dillworth blow. The trail boss lunged at Gabe, but once again Gabe was too quick for him, sidestepping out of the lumbering man's way. A look of rage suffused Dillworth's face as he swung wildly with both hands, managing only to land a glancing blow on Gabe's right bicep.

Gabe danced backward, his fists raised, feinting as he went. Dillworth followed him. Then the trail boss, his nostrils flaring as he breathed heavily, suddenly seized the cracker barrel sitting on the ground by the chuck wagon and raised it high above his head. Before Gabe could get out of the way, Dillworth brought the barrel crashing down on Gabe's head, knocking his hat off, and splitting the skin in the center of his skull. Gabe went down on his knees as barrel staves fell in a wooden shower all around him. He shook his head, trying to banish the red glare and flashing white lights in front of his eyes.

He heard Dillworth grunting and got to his feet just in time to avoid the barrel stave the trail boss had picked up from the ground and was bringing down toward his head. Gabe, fury flowing hot within him now, lunged at the advancing Dillworth and tore the stave from the man's hand. He tossed it aside, and his cocked right fist struck Dillworth squarely on the jaw, knocking his teeth together with an audible "clack."

Dillworth delivered a weak blow that caught Gabe squarely in the chest and another one which plowed into his gut. Gabe sucked air into his burning lungs. Ignoring the pain shrieking in his hands from the blows he had delivered, he moved in on Dillworth. He pummeled the man with a series of savage blows. The trail boss fought back, but Gabe could see that the man was weakening. Pressing his advantage, he continued pounding Dillworth.

The trail boss managed to connect with another blow to Gabe's heavily muscled gut that did no damage. He drew back his right fist and sent it flying toward Gabe's face. Gabe nimbly danced sideways, and the blow missed him. Its force carried Dillworth forward and, as the man went past him, Gabe raised both fists, interlocked the fingers of both hands, and then swung them together in a wide arc. The club of his linked fists slammed into the back of Dillworth's neck, sending him staggering a few paces. He stumbled over the tongue of the chuck wagon and went down. He lay on the ground, his hands clawing at the grass. His shoulders rose. His head hung down. He tried to pull himself up, but his legs gave way and he sprawled again on the ground, his face buried in the grass.

Gabe stood there, waiting. His breath was gusting in and out of his lips, and his chest was heaving like an overworked bellows.

He wasn't sure how much time had passed before Dillworth managed to get to his knees and then push himself erect. The trail boss turned to face him.

Panting through open lips, the lower one of which had been cut and was painting his teeth red, he said, in a voice that grated, "You're through here, Conrad."

Gabe wasn't surprised by the remark; he had been expecting it.

"Go herd Chickasaw cattle," Dillworth muttered. "You belong there, not here. Take your Indian friend and get the hell out of this white man's camp and don't come back."

Dillworth, swaying unsteadily, turned bleary eyes on Wolf who was still holding Curly hostage. "You!" he said, making the word sound like an obscenity. "You get out of here, too!"

"I want Carmody," Wolf said.

"Then go find him," Dillworth snarled. "As for the twenty-five dollar permit to cross Chickasaw territory and the fifteen cents per head grazing fee you say I've got to pay, you'll have to wait till I get authorization from the cattle owners in Texas."

"I'm not known as a patient man, Dillworth," Wolf warned. "I'll give you just two more days to come up with the money. After that time, if you haven't . . ." He let his words trail away.

Letting go of Curly who promptly sprinted away from him, Wolf went over to Gabe and said, "It's time we got out of here, my friend." He holstered his gun as Gabe retrieved his own gun and hat. Looping Gabe's right arm over his shoulder and holding tightly to it, he helped Gabe walk away from the cow camp toward where they had left their horses in the woods.

Behind them, jeers and catcalls from the drovers filled the air. Words reached them, ugly words like "heathen" and "uncivilized savage" and "Conrad, the Indian lover."

"I didn't mean to cause you all this trouble," Wolf said to Gabe.

"You didn't cause it; Dillworth did."

"Feisty fellow, that Dillworth."

"Not feisty enough. I downed him."

"That you did. He's not likely to forget the beating you gave him in any kind of a hurry."

"He ought to consider himself a lucky man."

"A lucky man?"

"All he got from me was a beating, not a bullet."

"What will you do now?" Wolf inquired as they reached their horses.

"You mean now that I just got fired from my drover's job?"

Wolf nodded.

"Well, I plan to stick around and lend you a hand in settling the Dillworth and Carmody matters if you'll have me."

"Have you? I'd be delighted to have you help us out. But as I said earlier, I feel somewhat guilty getting you involved in this problem in the first place. If I hadn't, you wouldn't have gotten into that fistfight back there."

"I'm doing this of my own free will. You're not making me do it."

"You can stay with me at my place if you like."

"That would suit me fine."

Both men climbed aboard their horses and moved out.

Later, when they arrived at Wolf's log cabin, which was not far from the one inhabited by Harley and Annie Sadler, they put their horses in a small shed behind the house, stripped their gear from them, rubbed them down, filled their feed bins, and then went inside the cabin.

"You hungry, Gabe?"

"Hungry enough to eat a bear. Raw."

"I'll cook something for us. Make some coffee."

As Wolf began to fire up the wood stove and make other preparations for the meal he planned to cook, Gabe looked around the cabin. Like the Sadlers' house, it was a typical Chickasaw dwelling consisting of a double log house with a

connection covered passageway. The furniture was wooden
and of a style termed "country" by many, hand-hewn and
held together by pegs rather than nails. There was a single
window containing glass but no curtain. The puncheon floor
was clean and so were the glass globes covering the two
lamps Wolf had lighted upon their arrival.

"You live here alone, do you?" Gabe asked the Lighthorseman who was slicing a piece of beef into chunks on
a carving board.

"Yes. This is the family homestead. My parents are
both dead, and my brother is back east studying to be a
lawyer."

The information about Wolf's brother took Gabe by
surprise. Wait a minute, he told himself. You're about
as bad as Dillworth and some of his drovers. How come
you're surprised that a Chickasaw would be studying law
at a university?

He knew that the Chickasaw tribe was composed of
mostly industrious individuals who, through hard work and
thrifty practices, had prospered. Many were wealthy here
and now in terms of real estate and other property such
as herds of cattle. So he shouldn't have been surprised to
learn that Wolf's brother was a university student.

Before putting the pot containing the chunks of beef
on the stove, Wolf tossed a small piece of meat into the
flames. When he noticed Gabe giving him a quizzical look,
he explained, "Throwing a piece of meat into the fire before
cooking a meal is an old Chickasaw custom. It's supposed
to be a means of producing temporal good things and of
averting those that are evil.

"I suspect it's related to the similar custom of currying
favor with our gods by offering them a choice piece of
flesh cut from the first deer slain on the winter and summer
hunts."

Wolf busied himself with the meal he was preparing, and
it wasn't long before he placed before Gabe a plate heaped
high with boiled beef, rice, and thick slices of brown bread.
He poured coffee into a cup and placed it at Gabe's elbow
before sitting down to his own meal.

Gabe ate hungrily, hardly taking time to chew the beef which turned out to be both tender and tasty, seasoned as it was with wild cinnamon. The rice was a bit too bland to suit Gabe's taste, but the strong pungent coffee made up for it.

He noticed that Wolf said little during their meal. The man was clearly preoccupied. As the Lighthorseman poured himself a second cup of coffee, Gabe said, "You're worried about that herd, aren't you?"

"Among other things," Wolf said with an air of distraction. "Chickasaw Nation and therefore the Lighthorsemen have, at the moment, more problems than a man can shake a stick at."

"Such as?"

Wolf leaned back in his chair. "Intruders who are illegally in the Nation for one. Most of them are white men. They're businessmen of one stripe or another, a lot of them, although there are also laborers and farm workers numbered among them. Some of the wealthier ones have built costly residences and the fact is they don't own the land their houses are built on. Chickasaw Nation does. A lot of them have never bothered to obtain permits from the Chickasaw government which allow male noncitizens to reside, do business, or labor in the Nation.

"We—the Chickasaw—are, in the opinion of many, running a real risk of being absorbed into a nonnative, or white, society. The Lighthorsemen, by the way, are charged with the duty of expelling such noncitizens who hold no residence permits. It's an overwhelming task. Probably one that can never be accomplished. There are too many of them and too few of us. Some of the whites have gone so far as to marry our women to keep from having to purchase residence permits and to gain, by means of their marriages, citizen status in the Nation.

"The police, I can tell you, have their hands full these days. An offshoot of the intruder problem is the one involving the Negroes residing in the Nation. There are thousands of them now."

"You're talking about the Chickasaws' former slaves?"

"No. Well, yes, I am. What I mean to say is that some of the Negroes are here legitimately as Chickasaw freedmen. But we never owned more than a thousand slaves in total. There are now an estimated five thousand Negroes claiming to be Chickasaw freedmen with legal status in the Nation. Most of them drifted up here from Texas after the war. Proving who is and who isn't a legitimate freedman is one more overwhelming task we're facing.

"On top of all that, there are the white cattlemen who come through our territory on their way to the railheads in Kansas. What the Nation needs to keep control of all this isn't just a police force like the Lighthorsemen but a veritable army."

"It's clear to see that you men have got your hands full." Gabe paused a moment before asking, "What are you planning to do about Dave Carmody and the rape charge against him?"

"I've been considering traveling up to Ardmore to try to find him, but the more I think about that prospect the more I come to believe it would amount to little more than a fool's errand. Ardmore's a pretty big town. Looking for Carmody there would be tantamount to looking for a will-o'-the-wisp in the woods."

"Chances are he'll be back with the herd when you return there to collect the money due the tribal treasury."

"I'm not so sure about that. He might, when Dillworth tells him about the rape charge pending against him, decide to take off for parts unknown. Maybe I really ought to go up to Ardmore and try to apprehend him there."

Wolf drank the last of the coffee in his cup before adding, "I'll sleep on it and make up my mind in the morning. You ready to turn in, Gabe?"

"Might as well."

"There's two bedrooms in the other cabin. You go out that door there, through the passage, and you'll find the one on the left's not occupied."

"I could help you clear up here."

"There's really no need to. I'll just wash up these few things and go to bed myself. Have a good night."

"See you in the morning."

Gabe got up from the table and made his way through the passage to the cabin containing his room for the night. He found a soft bed against one of its walls and stretched out on it with a sigh. He shifted position several times because, despite the softness of the bed's mattress, he still suffered from aches and pains scattered throughout his body which were the legacy of his fight with Dillworth.

He made himself as comfortable as possible and lay there on his back gazing out of the room's one window at the moon sailing in the sky, his hands clasped behind his head. He went over in his mind the discussion he had had with Wolf at the supper table. It was certainly true that Wolf and the rest of the Chickasaw Lighthorsemen had more than their fair share of problems to solve. Well, maybe he could help them solve one of them at least. Namely, the problem with Dillworth arising from Wolf's attempts to impose Chickasaw law upon the trail boss and the herd he was driving north.

He certainly intended to help try to solve that problem. It had become for him a matter of personal pride. He felt that he owed it to Annie Sadler and to Wolf, both of whom, as Indians, had been treated with contempt by Dillworth and the white men traveling with him. That knowledge rankled within him. He felt he would not be able to rest easy until he had helped right the wrong that had been done to Annie Sadler by Dave Carmody and had seen to it that Dillworth and his men—illegal intruders in Chickasaw Nation—were made to pay the lawful price for their intrusion.

Wolf could use all the help he could get. With that thought in mind, Gabe found himself thinking of his own upbringing among another band of Indians—the Oglala, or the People, as they called themselves. What would a man of the People do in such circumstances? he asked himself. Fight, was the answer that came to him. As I'm going to do for what's right. Maybe that man of the People would also offer up a prayer for help. Not only to the supreme being, *Wakan-Tanka*, but also to Whope, one of the Associate Gods of the People. Whope, whom the People

called the Beautiful One. Whope daughter of the Sun and
Moon, who served as the Great Mediator and as the patron
of harmony and pleasure. Maybe Whope was the one to
turn to in the hope that she could help establish harmony
between Dillworth and the Chickasaws where now there
was nothing but discord. He silently uttered her name and
then whispered some prayerful words into the darkness.

An hour later, he was still awake. Still tossing and turning
in the bed. He had heard Jackson Wolf enter the room next
door to his some time ago. No sound came from that
room now. He knew his restlessness was not a result of
the fistfight or his angry thoughts about Dillworth. There
was a yearning within him that demanded satisfaction. He
had begun with his recollection of the soft eyes and lovely
lips of Annie Sadler. It had grown steadily as he lay in the
bed staring out the window at the moon.

Giving up on his attempts to sleep, he got up and went
outside. The night, he found, had cooled down somewhat,
but there was still the heady warmth of summer in the air.
It was borne on a breeze that was as restless as he was. He
paced back and forth in front of the cabin, his hands thrust
deep into his pockets.

Annie Sadler, in memory, strolled by his side. He left
the cabin and walked some distance away from it, stopping when the Sadler homestead came into view in the
distance. It was a lumpish dark shadow in the night. No
light burned in any of its windows. Annie was probably
sleeping. The very thought aroused him as he imagined her
lying in bed.

The yearning within him grew stronger, if that were
possible. It dominated his thoughts and set his scalp to
tingling.

He was about to turn away and head back to the Wolf
cabin when something in the distance attracted his attention.
At first, he wasn't really sure he had seen anything. But
then, as he continued watching the spot where he thought he
had seen movement, he saw her. Annie Sadler was moving
slowly, almost languidly, through the night. She was barely
visible because of the shadows shed by the trees beneath

which she was walking as she headed for the hummock on the side of the homestead.

Gabe did not hesitate. He began to make his way toward her, resisting the impulse to run. If he were to come sprinting up to her, he was sure he would startle her. He didn't want to do that. He wanted to . . .

He quickened his pace.

When he was still some distance away from her, he called her name. Softly, but urgently.

She turned quickly in his direction, so quickly in fact that her long black hair swirled in front of her face. She reached up and in a nervous but delicate gesture pulled it aside.

"Who—" she began.

Before she could complete her question, Gabe was standing beside her. "I was up at Jackson Wolf's cabin," he told her, speaking softly because Annie looked as if she were about to bolt. "I saw you walking out."

"It's you."

He gave her a reassuring smile.

"I wasn't sure I would ever see you again."

"Well, here I am."

"Did you—did Jackson—arrest that man?"

"Wolf and me, we went to the cow camp, but he wasn't there. It turned out the trail boss had sent him to Ardmore on an errand." Gabe, noting Annie's crestfallen expression, hurriedly added, "But we'll get him. Wolf told me tonight that he's thinking of heading to Ardmore to see if maybe he can't find him up there."

When Annie wrapped her arms around herself and turned away, Gabe took a step closer to her. "What's wrong? You cold?"

"No," she said, but he was sure he had seen her shiver. "It's just that I don't feel really safe knowing that man is still on the loose. I'm afraid he might come back."

"He won't," Gabe said with more confidence than he actually felt.

Annie tightened her grip on herself. "I was afraid to come out here tonight. For hours, I didn't. But then I told myself that I couldn't live like an animal in a cage. An animal that was afraid of what would happen to it if it dared to try to live a normal life free of fear."

"You don't have to be afraid now. I'm here."

Annie gave him a glance and then looked away again. "I was going to the top of the hummock."

"To your favorite place."

"Yes."

"Would you mind all that much if I were to go up there with you?"

Gabe was disappointed to notice a moment's hesitation on Annie's part. But then she said, "No, I wouldn't mind."

As she set out for the hummock, Gabe took up a position by her side. Together they climbed the low hill until they were standing atop it in the moon's pale light.

"Isn't the night wonderful?" Annie asked. "It's so soft and gentle." Her voice trailed away. Then, after a moment, without looking directly at Gabe, she asked, "What happened at the cow camp?"

Gabe wasn't sure how to answer her question. Nor was he sure about what it was she really wanted to know. Was it that she wanted to learn whether or not he and Wolf had received cooperation from Dillworth and the others? Or did she want to be assured that the cow camp encounter would lead to the apprehension and confinement of Dave Carmody? He decided to do the only thing he felt he could do. He decided to tell her the truth.

"The trail boss, a man named Dillworth, didn't believe that Dave Carmody had done what you claim he did."

Annie's eyes widened. Her mouth worked but at first no words came. Then they came in a rush. "He did! I told you—and Jackson when Grandpapa first sent for him—the truth!"

"I know you did. But Dillworth was skeptical. He went so far as to suggest that maybe you accused Dave Carmody for reasons of your own and Carmody never really did— what you say he did."

"I don't understand. How could I make the claim I did against a man I had never seen before in my life?"

"You and your grandfather drove past the herd on your way home. Dillworth thinks you saw Carmody and later claimed he had raped you."

"I never saw Dave Carmody when we drove past the herd. I never saw him until he came here that night. But even if I had seen him, why would I say he raped me if he hadn't done so?"

"Dillworth suggested that maybe you're pregnant and are trying not to make trouble for whoever's the father of your baby."

"Me. With child?" Annie's expression grew first incredulous, then stern. "That's not true."

"I told him his theory sounded pretty preposterous to me."

"Carmody's going to get away with it, isn't he?"

"Not if Wolf and me have anything to say about it, he's not."

"I am so ashamed."

"There's no need to be. What happened to you wasn't your fault."

"But it happened. I can't forget that fact. I will never forget that fact. It will haunt me for the rest of my life. Whenever I look at a man, I will see *that* man, Dave Carmody."

"Annie, that doesn't have to be." Gabe took a step closer to her. "Not all men are like Carmody. Some of us can be kind and very gentle." He reached out and took her hand.

She flinched and tried to free her hand, but he held it firmly as he gazed into her eyes.

"If you let that one bad apple spoil the whole barrelful, your life's going to turn out to be an empty wasteland where nothing will grow but bitterness born of regret. I'm not much good at advising other people about what they ought to do, but it seems to me, for what it's worth, that you've got to put what happened behind you and go on."

"How can I do that?"

"It might not be the easiest thing in the world to do, but I think it can be done. You might have to work hard at it at first, but over time it'll get easier. You probably won't believe me now, but in time chances are you'll have trouble remembering Dave Carmody's name. He'll fade, along with his name, from your mind."

"I don't believe that. I'll never forget his name—or him."

"Well, maybe you're right, though I do doubt it." Gabe took Annie's other hand in his. "You're one beautiful woman, but then I suppose you know that. I'd hate to see such beauty spoiled, and that's what'll happen if you let Carmody win out over you."

"What do you mean?"

"He wins if you hold fast to your hate for him. Oh, I know how hard you must hate him at the moment. But hate, it's a funny thing. It's like a plant that can only grow in a desert. It flourishes where the sun blasts the ground it grows on and where next to no rain falls to lighten the soil and turn things green and pretty. Hate makes a person harsh. Before long, it etches lines in a person's face—around the eyes and the mouth. Hate has a way of setting a person's teeth to grinding together and emptying a person's eyes of all else save its own black self. When hate takes to thriving in a person, there's no room left in them anymore for mercy or pity. Certainly not for love. And that, to my way of thinking, is one sad and sorry state of affairs."

Annie stared at Gabe, her brow furrowing. He returned her steady gaze and added to it the trace of a smile. Moments passed in which he could see Annie weighing what he had said, wondering if it might be true. When a smile as faint as his own lifted the corners of her lips and moonlight danced in her eyes, he let go of her hands and put his arms around her.

Her body stiffened and then began to tremble. She pulled away from him, breaking his embrace.

He let her go but said softly, "Every man you meet from now on won't be Dave Carmody. I'm not. Please don't tar us all with the same brush, Annie."

When a strangled sob escaped her lips, he reached out and drew her close to him. She was still trembling, but now that trembling was a result of the sobs that racked her body as she wept uncontrollably. He continued to hold her as she rested a cheek against his chest and her tears dampened his shirt.

"Thank you for trying to help me," she murmured minutes later when her tears and sobs had subsided. She raised her head and looked up at Gabe. "You make me dare to hope that there is a good life ahead for me despite Carmody and what he did to me."

"There is," Gabe assured her. "There surely is. All you have to do is reach out and grab hold of it."

Annie put her arms around him and squeezed.

Gabe hugged her to him and then bent his head and lightly kissed her neck. This time the contact brought no stiffening of her body. No withdrawal. Emboldened by those facts, he cupped her chin in one hand, raised her head, and kissed her again—squarely on the lips this time.

At first, she simply accepted his kiss. But then, as their lips remained locked together, she began to respond. First, her grip on his body tightened. Then her lips pressed eagerly against his. Finally, her lips parted, and she eagerly accepted his thrusting tongue.

Annie moaned as their lips parted, her eyes closed, her face remaining uptilted as if waiting expectantly for another kiss. Gabe obliged. This time it was her tongue which breached the barrier of his lips and teeth.

Then suddenly, Annie withdrew from him. She began to fumble with her clothes. Bows and buttons gave way under her flying fingers. She let her skirt fall. Then her chemise. She took off her printed muslin blouse and let it fall on top of her skirt and chemise.

Gabe was naked only a few minutes later. He eased her down upon the grass, reminding himself to be gentle and tender.

CHAPTER EIGHT

"I've decided to go up to Ardmore," Jackson Wolf announced the next morning when he and Gabe had finished their breakfast in the Lighthorseman's cabin.

"I'll go with you," Gabe volunteered.

But Wolf shook his head. "I can handle Carmody myself—if I should happen to run him to ground in Ardmore. But there is something you can do for me, if you will."

"What is it?"

"Stand in for me today in the game of toli that will be played as part of the busk festival."

"Toli? What kind of game's that?"

"Have you ever heard of the old Indian game called baggataway?"

"Yes. It's like the game lacrosse that the Canadians play."

"That's right, it is. Only in toli, two rackets instead of one are used. Everything else though is pretty much the same. The court's about five hundred feet long. The object of the game is to get the ball through the upright goal posts at the ends of the court without touching it with your hands—only with your rackets. Each goal counts as one point. At the end of the game, whichever team has the most points wins. If there's a tie, the game goes on until the tie is broken.

"My team is composed of members of the *Koishto* clan, the Panther clan. Today we are to play against the *Shawi* or Raccoon clan. There's been a strong rivalry between our two clans for a number of years. The reason I'm asking you to take my place is it would shame my clan if I do not play or provide a substitute to take my place."

"I'll stand in for you if that's what you want, but I've got to tell you that I'm not sure how good I'll be at toli. I might wind up disgracing you and your Panther clan. It's been a long time since I played shinny."

"Shinny? Isn't that the name of a game played by the Oglala?"

Gabe put down the coffee cup he had been about to drink from and stared at it. He hesitated a moment before answering, "Yes."

"You've played shinny?"

"I have." Gabe looked up and met Wolf's penetrating gaze. "I was thinking that toli sounds a lot like shinny, and the word shinny slipped out on me. In shinny you're not allowed to touch the ball with your hands. You kick it. As in toli, each goal counts for one point."

Wolf said nothing, but Gabe knew the man had questions on his mind. He decided to answer them. He had gone this far. He might as well go all the way.

"I was raised among the Oglala. I lived with them until I was fourteen. My mother and I had been taken captive by them. When I was fourteen, my mother decided it was time for me to learn the ways of the white world. She made me leave the People. I didn't want to, but she insisted. So I left."

Wolf sat there absorbing the information Gabe had just given him for several silent minutes. Then, with a smile, he said, "You ought to be good at toli since it's so much like shinny. Playing toli will be like old times for you, I daresay."

"It seems I never can escape my past. It keeps cropping up to confront me in the darnedest places and at the darnedest times. Like now."

"I have a feeling you don't really want to escape your

past. Nor should you want to, in my humble opinion. The Oglala are a fine people."

"You're right. On both counts."

"Want some more coffee?"

"No, thanks. When does this game of toli begin?"

"Sometime today. There are more serious matters to tend to first as part of the festival. The new fire must be struck and sanctified. There is the rite of purging. The busk festival is ordained by the Chickasaw's Supreme Being, *Ababinili*, whom we conceive of as a composite force consisting of the Four Beloved Things Above—the Sun, Clouds, Clear Sky and He That Lives in the Clear Sky. It is a time for the renewal and perpetuation of health, as we see it. The busk, or green corn festival is held every year at the beginning of the first new moon after the green corn is ripe."

"Well, I'll do my best to help the Panther clan win."

"I expect you'll find playing toli today like old times with the Oglala."

Gabe nodded. "Like old—and good—times."

They were just finishing clearing away the remains of their breakfast when a loud knock sounded on the door. Wolf opened it and admitted the two men standing outside.

"Come on, Jackson," the burlier of the two cried, slapping Wolf on the back. "The doings are just about to start."

"You ready to whip the Raccoons' tails, Jackson?" the other more wiry man inquired with a gleam in his black eyes.

"I'm not playing toli today," Wolf declared.

His announcement brought dismay to the faces of his two visitors.

"You're not playing?" they chorused together. "Why not?"

"I have important Lighthorsemen business to attend to. But don't despair, my friends. I've got a man to take my place. This fellow is Gabe Conrad. Gabe, this barn-shouldered fellow's name is Harry Coffer and this skinny-as-a-snake—"

"But strong as an ox," the thin man interrupted with a grin.

"—is Amos Owens," Wolf concluded, completing the introductions.

Gabe shook hands with Coffer and Owens.

"You've played toli before?" Owens asked.

Gabe was about to admit that he hadn't when Wolf answered for him. "He'll help you boys win, I guarantee it."

Seeing the doubtful expressions on his visitors' faces, Wolf added, "Don't discount him just because he's white. He doesn't play with the color of his skin."

The doubt on the faces of Owens and Coffer was displaced by expressions of chagrin.

"We didn't mean—" Coffer began but was interrupted by Wolf.

"Let's go join the party," the Lighthorseman said.

The three men had no sooner emerged from the cabin when a long drum began to sound as a drummer seated cross-legged on the ground began to pound it with a heavy wooden stick. The rhythm of the man's drumming was somber, almost ominous.

Gabe and the others joined the crowd of Indians that was gathering in a glade some distance away where the drummer was making his music. They watched in silence as two men, imposing figures both, took up positions in the center of the glade where a small fire burned in a shallow clay bowl sitting on the ground. Both men wore mantles of white swan feathers and were attended by several other younger men.

"The men wearing the warriors' mantles," Wolf said to Gabe in a low tone, "are the *Hopaye*, which means Beloved Holy Men in our language. The others are lesser priests. The Hopaye are chosen, one each, from the two grand divisions of the Chickasaw tribe—the *Imosaktca* and the *Intcukwalipa*."

One of the young priests picked up the clay bowl and placed it on a bare wooden altar. The two holy men approached it, one on either side of the altar. One of them bent down and began to blow on the fire. From the other side of the altar, the other holy man did the same. Finally, as a result of their efforts, the old fire was extinguished. Then, with kindling provided by the attending priests, the holy men used a flint to strike a new fire on the ashes of the old.

As its flames flickered and then flared up, the watching Chickasaws began to cheer. Their cheering continued as the holy men fed tobacco, button snakeroot, and several ears of the new corn to the fresh flames.

As the new fire, now sanctified, burned brightly, the people formed into a line and approached the altar carrying their personal charms and medicine bundles to be blessed by the holy men.

As Gabe watched the progress of the religious ceremony, Annie Sadler appeared at the edge of the glade. He was about to go to her but, when she joined the line of people seeking blessings, he stayed where he was. Below her knee-length blue cotton dress she wore beaded strands of buffalo hair on her legs as ornaments. Gabe was surprised to notice that she carried in her hands a gleaming hunting knife with a horn handle.

His eyes remained on Annie as the people in the line moved along. He was still watching her when she held up the knife in her hand to be blessed by the priests. When the blessing had been given, she turned and left the altar, slipping the hunting knife into a leather sheath that hung from a belt she wore cinched around her slender waist.

When Gabe waved to her, she changed course and came toward him.

"Good morning," she said when she reached him.

"Good morning. Nice seeing you again."

Annie greeted Wolf and the two men with him and then stood next to Gabe as they all watched the blessing ceremony continue.

"I'll be back," Wolf told his companions. He pulled a medicine bundle from his pocket. "I'm going to get this blessed. Maybe the blessing of the Hopaye will bring me luck in my hunt for Carmody."

When he had gone to join the line snaking its way toward the holy men, Annie turned to Gabe. "Jackson is going after Carmody?"

"Yes. He's heading up to Ardmore where Carmody might or might not be. Wolf's decided to go up there and have a look around, see if he can find the man."

"You're going with him?"

Gabe shook his head. "No, I'm staying here. He asked me to take his place in the game of toli that's to be played some time today."

"It will take place after the purging."

"Purging?"

"We partake of a drink that the priests prepare. It is meant to purge all evil from our bodies. It makes one vomit after having drunk it."

"Doesn't sound very appetizing."

"It isn't meant to be. Strong medicine is needed to drive out evil."

Gabe and Annie stood with Coffer and Owens and watched as Wolf reached the priests and held up his medicine bundle. He bowed his head during the blessing and then, when it was completed, he left the altar.

"What have you got in that thing?" Gabe asked him when he had rejoined the others.

Wolf opened the bundle and held it out for Gabe to see.

Inside were several small white bones and two spotted and striated stones.

"This is what keeps me hale and hearty," Wolf said, pocketing his medicine bundle. "Or so I choose to believe."

"May it continue to do so," Annie said solemnly.

"It's time I was leaving," Wolf said. "I wish you luck during the game, Gabe."

"He'll need it," Coffer commented. "So will we all. Those men of the Raccoon clan are one rough bunch."

"It's time for the purging," Owens declared when Wolf had gone. "You coming Annie? Gabe?"

"Yes," Annie answered and glanced at Gabe.

"I'll go with you," he told her, "but I think I'll pass on the purging."

He walked with his three companions across the glade to where the priests had taken up a position at a table that stood beneath a towering locust tree. On it was a huge bowl and a number of cups. Gabe stood to one side as Annie and the two men helped themselves to cups which they filled with some of the dark liquid taken from the bowl. Each of them promptly drank, emptying their cups. Each of them then turned aside, walked some distance away and vomited.

When Annie had rejoined Gabe, she said, "Amos and Harry have gone to see some friends of theirs. They said they will come for you when it is time to play toli."

"What is in that drink you all just downed?"

"It contains boiled red root. We fast the night before we drink it." Annie made a face. "It's truly terrible to the taste, I must admit."

"I saw you in the line for the blessing. Is it common practice among the Chickasaws to get their holy men to bless knives?"

Annie shook her head. "No, it is not, I must confess. Mostly people take to the priests their charms and amulets and medicine bundles as Jackson did."

"But you took a knife. Do you mind my asking why?"

"I wanted the holy men to give power to this weapon of mine." Annie patted the knife that hung in its sheath on her hip. "Now that it has the power, I will use it to kill Dave Carmody if he ever comes near me again."

Gabe gave Annie an appraising glance.

"You do not believe me?"

"Oh, I believe you all right. I was just wondering if you know what you're doing."

"I know what I'm doing. This knife is my shadow fighting knife. It is part of my personal medicine. When I die, it will be interred with me so that I may use it to fight off any enemies I meet while on my way to the world of the spirits. Meanwhile, it will serve me as a weapon against my enemies in this world.

"Look, the dancing begins," Annie remarked, abruptly changing the subject.

Men and women were moving into the center of the

glade as the log drum was joined by other instruments—
rattles made of gourds and hand-carved wooden flutes.
Many members of both sexes wore turtle-shell rattles bound
about their knees.

The rattling of the turtle shells and the gourds rose in
strength until it almost drowned out the drumming. But
the log drum managed to hold its own as it increased
its beat to a rapid rhythm that set the people's feet to
dancing. The flute sent a shrill wave of thin sound into
the air that rode atop the drumbeats and wove its way in
and out of the rattling, sometimes in an almost ear-piercing
manner.

Annie pointed to the dancers. "They are doing the buffalo
dance."

Gabe watched as the men, their bodies bent forward and
their index fingers pointing forward from the sides of their
heads, danced the role of the bull buffalos. They lunged
at one another, feinted, withdrew. Then they circled the
women, kicking up dirt with their feet that they pretended
were hooves as they simulated rutting buffalo bulls.

The women, the cows, alternately advanced and fled
from the bulls, the men.

Annie looked up at Gabe as he stood by her side. She
took his hand and, without speaking a word, led him in
among the dancers. She became almost immediately trans-
formed as her feet began to pound the ground and her body
swayed to the rising rhythm being produced by the drum
and other instruments. She cocked her head to one side.
She held out her arms to Gabe.

But when he reached for her, she turned and danced away
from him. He lowered his head, bent his body at the waist
and went after her, taking slow steady steps which, as he
came closer to her, became quick and sure. He circled her,
using his fingers to simulate buffalo horns, his eyes glued
to her seductively undulating body.

She thrust her pelvis at him. He sprang toward her. She
let him get within inches of her before nimbly sidestepping
and dancing away from him again. He followed her, his
breath coming in short sharp gusts and sounding for all

the world, he thought, like the snorting of a rutting buffalo bull. As he danced the buffalo dance with Annie, he recalled their coming together of the night before. Remembered the heat of their bodies as they melded in sweet union. Felt his blood burning in his veins as his thoughts caught fire.

The music thrummed in his ears. The flute wailed and the drum somberly sounded. The rattles in the hands of the musicians and those tied to the legs of many of the dancers clattered in his mind along with the raging lust that had taken possession of him at the rousing sight of Annie dancing before him and luring him on in the way of females everywhere, no matter the species, be it buffalo cow or woman.

A whoop went up from somewhere. It had been louder than the instruments and had seemed to challenge them. Another whoop followed the first.

Gabe, his concentration on Annie and on his role as a buffalo bull broken, turned his head and saw the source of the two wild whoops.

Harley Sadler was dancing—if that's what his erratic movements could be called. Gabe thought it amazing that the man was able to remain upright. He swooped and swayed unsteadily. Clearly, the man was not just caught up in the excitement of the dance and its symbolic mating ritual. The man was obviously drunk.

Sadler's eyes were unfocused and red-rimmed. His hands shook but not with the movements of the dance. He stumbled, miraculously recovered his balance, stumbled again.

A male dancer tried to take his arm and lead him away, but Sadler shook the man off and continued his eccentric, almost violent gyrations.

Gabe suddenly became aware that Annie had stopped dancing and was moving among the dancers as she made her way toward her grandfather whose gray hair was flying about his contorted face as he spun in a clumsy circle. He noted the stricken expression on her face and the tears welling in her eyes.

He went after her. When he caught up with her, she was pleading with her grandfather to go home. But Sadler was shaking his head vigorously from side to side while continuing to dance.

"Come on ever'body!" he called out as he took a bottle from his hip pocket. "Ever'body have a good goddamn time, hear?"

He uncorked the bottle and drank thirstily from it. He danced a few steps, still calling stridently to the dancers to "have a good goddamn time."

"Grandpapa," Annie said, reaching for the bottle, "you've had enough for now. Let's go home."

Sadler lowered the bottle and gave his granddaughter a bleary-eyed glare. "Go home? Don't be silly. This is the busk festival!"

Annie flinched as if he had struck her. But she persisted in her efforts to get her grandfather to leave. Under the staring eyes of the no longer dancing men and women, she whispered to him and tried to get a grip on his waist.

He shook her hand off and drained the bottle. Then he stared gloomily at it. Shook it. Put it once more to his lips. Cursed. Flung the empty bottle to the ground where it smashed to smithereens against a stone.

"Annie, I need money," he whined, no longer dancing, only his lips and his eyes moving. "I bought that—" he pointed to the broken bottle on the ground—"with the last of the money you gave me yesterday."

"Grandpapa, you promised me you wouldn't spend that money on alcohol."

"I tried not to," Sadler moaned. "I did. But I couldn't keep my promise. Annie, give me some money."

"No, Grandpapa. No more money."

"No more money?" Sadler repeated, his eyes pleading with Annie. When she shook her head in blunt denial of his request, he muttered an oath. "You ungrateful little bitch!" he screamed at her. "I took you in when you had no place to go and now you turn on me like an unnatural child!"

"Come, Grandpapa, I'll take you home," Annie said, her face flushing with embarrassment. "You can rest—"

"Don't want to rest. Want to drink." Sadler staggered a few paces, almost colliding with Gabe. "Oh, it's you," he muttered. He was about to step around Gabe when a thought seemed to strike him. His eyes narrowed as he gazed at Gabe. "I'll wager you wouldn't turn down a man in desperate need, would you, Conrad?"

"Let's get you home, Mr. Sadler," Gabe said.

Sadler pulled back from Gabe. "Don't touch me. Just give me—lend me—some money. Anything you can spare. I'll pay it back, I promise you. My word is my bond. Ask anybody. They'll tell you. Harley Sadler, former Principal Chief of the noble Chickasaw tribe is—"

Sadler lapsed into silence. He frowned and shook his head as if to clear it. "What was I saying?" he asked no one in particular. Then, to Gabe he said with a lopsided smile. "I remember. You were offering to lend me some money. How much did you have in mind?"

Instead of answering the question, Gabe stepped forward and in one fluid movement, lifted Sadler off the ground and slung him over his shoulder. He gestured to Annie who led the way out of the glade. Behind them, he heard some of the Chickasaws snickering.

Neither he nor Annie spoke as they made their way toward the Sadler homestead. But Sadler shouted threats against both Gabe and his granddaughter as he weakly pounded Gabe's lower back with his fists.

"Put me down, dammit!" he bellowed in a whiskey-coarsened voice. "Help! Somebody help an old man! I'm being kidnapped!"

And then he lost consciousness.

Gabe continued carrying his burden, saying nothing, as Sadler's limply hanging arms bounced against his body and the man began to snore.

When he reached the homestead, Annie opened the door and led Gabe to Sadler's bedroom where he unburdened himself of the old man, laying him gently down upon his rope bed.

Annie covered her grandfather with a quilt and then she and Gabe left the bedroom.

"I don't know what I'm going to do about him," Annie said as they entered the kitchen and sat down across from one another at a table in the center of the room. "He's not a bad man. But when he drinks there's just no telling what he will do."

"It's never a pretty sight when the red-eye gets a good firm grip on a man. When that happens, it's a slippery, one-way ride downhill with a hard landing when a fellow hits bottom."

"I wish there was something I could do."

"Don't give him money."

"I tried that for a time. I had to give it up. I couldn't stand the way he would beg me for money. The way he would humble—almost degrade—himself before me while wheedling the money out of me so he could go and buy liquor and drink himself into a stupor."

"Tell the people where he buys his booze about the problem you're having. Tell them not to sell it to him anymore."

"I did do that. They cooperated. But Grandpapa just went farther afield to buy what he seems to need so desperately. He is bound and determined to get it, and so far he has always managed to do so. Gabe, I'm afraid of him."

Annie looked out the window, her upper teeth biting her lower lip. "Just last week, he went on a rampage after drinking I don't know how much liquor that he managed to obtain somewhere although I didn't give him the money to buy it. I think he must have borrowed the money to buy it. Or perhaps he stole it. He ranted and raved, and when I tried to quiet him down, he—hit me.

"I couldn't help myself. I began to cry." Annie turned to face Gabe. There was the trace of a smile on her face. "He immediately repented what he had done. He even begged my forgiveness. He was like a little boy who had been naughty and was quite thoroughly ashamed of himself over his misdeeds. It was really quite amusing in one way and charming in another."

"There's nothing funny nor charming about a drunk," Gabe said bluntly, his words wiping the smile from Annie's face. "Drunks can be mean or they can be sloppily sentimental. But they can never, it seems, be honest and forthright with the people who love them. They cheat. They lie.

Annie, honey, I think you ought to consider putting some distance between you and your grandpa."

"Oh, I couldn't leave him! That is what you meant, isn't it? That I should leave here and him?"

"That's exactly what I meant. And you can do it. All you have to do is make up your mind to change your life and the next step's easy. It's that making-up-your-mind part that's the hardest step to take. Annie, I'm worried about you. I'm worried about what he might take it into his head to do to you when he's under the influence."

"Oh, Grandpapa would never do anything to hurt me."

"Maybe not when he's sober. But you said yourself just now that he hit you. Honey, you're starting to step into the same trap the old man's already caught in. You sound to me like you won't face up to the truth of what your life has become. That can be downright dangerous, if not fatal."

Annie again turned to gaze out of the window as if out there, among the trees and the sunlight, she might find a way out of her dilemma. "You may be right," she said tentatively.

"I am right. You know I am."

She nodded. And then started, half-rising from her chair, as a choked cry came from the other room.

"Stay put," Gabe told her. "I'll go see to him."

When Gabe returned, Annie was sitting stiffly and expectantly in her chair. "He's alright. He must have had a nightmare. He's still asleep."

"He'll sleep for hours now. It's a chance for me to have a little peace."

Gabe went to Annie and raised her up from her chair. "This is no way for you to live. I want you to promise me that you'll think about ways to change your life for the better. I want you to promise me that you'll stop worrying about the old man and start taking better care of yourself. Before something bad happens to you."

"Nothing bad will happen to me, I'm sure of it."

"Are you?"

Annie was silent.

"Will you promise me?"

She hesitated for a long moment and then answered. "Yes. Yes, I will."

"What do you say we go back to the busk festival now? My feet feel as if they're far from finished dancing. How about yours?"

Annie took the arm Gabe offered her and together they left the cabin and started walking back to the glade where the celebration was taking place.

On the way, they met Coffer and Owens coming toward them.

"Gabe," Owens said as they met, "we came after you. The game's about to begin."

"We saw you leave with Annie and the old chief," Coffer said. "Is everything alright?"

"My Grandpapa is sleeping," Annie answered.

"You going to play toli with us as planned, Gabe?" Owens asked. "Without a full team, we'd be disqualified."

"You bet your boots I'm going to play," Gabe assured the two men. "Like I said before though, I don't know how much good I'm going to do for your Panther clan. But I'll do my best."

"Come on then," Owens said, clapping Gabe on the back.

The three men, with Annie following, made their way back to the glade where a game was already in progress.

"That's toli?" Gabe asked, puzzled. "That's not the way Wolf described it to me."

"No, that's a game called akabatle," Owens explained. "Women as well as men play it. Our turn at toli's coming up next."

Gabe stood with the others and watched the men and women who were chasing a ball made from a scraped and stuffed piece of deerskin and sewed with deer sinew across the court where the game of toli was also to be played. When one of the players got his or her hands on the ball, that person threw it at the effigy of a man made of sticks bound with rawhide. The figure had a vividly painted face and was perched atop a tall pole set in the center of the court.

"Missed," Owens said under his breath as one of the men threw the ball and it sailed harmlessly past the effigy.

A woman on the other side of the pole supporting the effigy caught the ball and threw it.

A loud cheer went up from the crowd as the ball struck the effigy and knocked it to one side.

Two more hits were scored in the next few minutes, one of them by the same woman who had just made the earlier hit.

When the game of akabatle finally ended the pole was removed from the center of the court and carried away by several men, the battered effigy dangling from it.

"Our position's on the south side of the court," Coffer told Gabe who left Annie and went with Coffer and Owens to join the other Chickasaw men who were forming a line at the south end of the court. When he reached them, he was given two rackets which vaguely resembled the ones used in the game of lacrosse in Canada.

"See that big fellow there?" Coffer pointed to a member of the Raccoon clan standing with his teammates at the north end of the court. "His name's Alexander. Watch out for him. He's a bruiser and has put more than one man out of the game in our other meets. Running into him is like running into a locomotive."

"I'll try to stay out of his way."

A man standing on the sidelines raised a tin whistle to his mouth and blew it. In response to the shrill sound, the Raccoons spread out into a straight line which matched the one already formed by the Panthers.

The man on the sidelines put his whistle to his mouth again, raised his hand, blew a blast, and dropped his hand.

Raccoons and Panthers raced toward each other and the ball that rested in the center of the court, the same ball that had been used in the previously played game of akabatle.

One of the Raccoons reached the ball first and swept it up in the racket he held in his left hand. He let it fly, and it was caught by a Raccoon on the far side of the court who ran with it until one of the Panthers managed to dislodge it from his racket and it fell to the ground. What followed was a scramble for possession of the ball in which several players on both sides landed in a heap on the ground.

But the ball had been scooped up by Gabe who went racing down the court toward the goal at the Raccoon's end of the court. He shook off the Raccoons who were pursuing him and threw the ball as hard as he could toward the goal posts.

But before it could sail between them, Alexander appeared out of nowhere and caught the ball in one of his rackets. He sprinted down the court, his head lowered. Gabe lunged for him, but Alexander managed to switch the ball from his right to his left racket, preventing Gabe from knocking the ball from his hand. Undeterred, Gabe turned and went racing after Alexander.

The Raccoons took up defensive positions on either side of their man, preventing any Panthers from getting close enough to him to make him lose possession of the ball. Alexander, with his flanking guards, passed the midpoint of the court and raced on.

Gabe's legs pumped and his heart pounded as he went after the Raccoons who were closing in on the Panther goal post. He plowed into the flankers on Alexander's left and had almost reached Alexander himself when the man raised his racket high above his head and threw the ball. It went soaring through the air between the goal posts, eliciting a cheer from some of the spectators who were supporters of the Raccoon clan.

On the next play, another Raccoon scored a second point, thanks in large part to the excellent interference run by the brawny Alexander, who bowled over two Panthers during the skirmish.

The Raccoons kept possession of the ball and almost scored a third goal on top of the first but Gabe, with help from Owens, carried the ball down the length of the court. Passing it from one man's racket to the next as each man ran on the outer edges of the court, they managed to keep the Panthers chasing back and forth between them in pursuit of the ball that spent most of its time airborne.

The goal Gabe scored at the end of that play brought applause from the fans of the Panthers and loud cries of encouragement, some of which took such forms as "Kill the Raccoons!" and "Eat 'em alive, Panthers!"

On the next play, Alexander sent Gabe flying head over heels as he deliberately collided with his opponent. With the wind knocked out of him, it took Gabe several minutes to regain his feet and get back in the game. The two teams were far down the field and close to the Panthers' goal post when he rejoined the play. He headed for Alexander who was taunting the Panthers at the top of his voice as he nimbly evaded them and tossed the ball back and forth between his two rackets.

Gabe shouldered a Raccoon out of his way and swung his racket in an attempt to snare the ball. But a wily Raccoon used his own racket to knock Gabe's aside. Alexander laughed scornfully. He was about to make the toss for another goal when Gabe repeated his maneuver and this time snared the ball with his racket as it bounced from one of Alexander's rackets to the other. Carrying the ball, Gabe sprinted, with Coffer running on his right, down the court toward the Raccoon's goal post.

As Alexander gained on him and then was almost on top of him, Coffer glanced over his shoulder, saw the furious Raccoon, and threw himself backward. His body collided head on with Alexander's. Both men went down.

Gabe ran on. A moment later, he scored again, evening up the match.

Among the cheers that greeted his goal, he thought he could distinguish Annie's voice. But, as play resumed, he had to admit to himself that he was only imagining the sound of her voice. He had only wished to hear her cheering him on. Still, as the game continued, he did manage to catch a glimpse of her standing among the spectators and jumping up and down like an excited schoolgirl. The sight of her gave him a renewed sense of purpose.

He ran interference for Owens who had taken possession of the ball and was running like an antelope toward the Raccoon's goal, the ball trapped firmly in his racket. When

Owens threw the ball in an attempt to score, it was inter-
cepted. The Raccoons ran it back toward the Panthers' goal
posts, tossing it from one of their players to another as
they went.

No Panther managed to get the ball away from them
despite the team's best efforts. The game continued with
neither team scoring a point. The crowd had become fren-
zied as they urged their teams on to victory. Then the
cheering grew less loud and came less often as the two
teams effectively blocked their opponents' attempts to score
a point and break the tie.

It was not until one of the Panthers, a man whose name
Gabe did not know, snared the ball as it was thrown from
one Raccoon to another and ran with it as if the world
behind him were coming to an end, that the tide began to
turn in favor of the Panthers. The Panther skirted a Raccoon
who came at him with killing in his eyes. He leaped over
a Raccoon who had stumbled in his path and came down
beyond the man and ran right on, his head twisting from
side to side as he looked back over his shoulders to see
where his pursuers were.

The Panther seemed to fly down the court. When he was
within twenty yards of the Raccoon's goal posts, his right
arm came up and he sent the ball whirling through the air.

The crowd screamed and clapped their hands—except for
the spectators siding with the Raccoons—as the ball sailed
between the goal posts and the sideline official's whistle
shrilled, signaling an end to the game.

Gabe went down under the combined weight of both
Coffer and Owens, both of whom gleefully jumped on
him while shouting their joy at the sky. Other Panthers
leaped on top of them. Congratulating one another as they
almost smothered one another, they finally all got to their
feet and raised their arms high above their heads to signal
their victory over the Raccoons who were sulking off the
court. Among them, Alexander was scowling. But, as he
passed Gabe, the man graciously stopped to shake hands
and say, "It was a sorry day for us when Jackson Wolf
dropped out and put you in his place. Jackson hasn't scored

a goal against the Raccoons in over a year. But here you come and score two. I'm going to look up our Chickasaw law to see if I can find a statute that'll keep a white man like you from playing toli."

He gave Gabe a grin and walked off the court.

He had no sooner done so than Annie appeared at Gabe's side. She embraced and congratulated him and then the other Panthers on their victory.

"It's time for the feasting," she told Gabe when they were alone. "Are you hungry?"

"I am that."

Annie led him under some trees at the edge of the glade where tables and benches had been set up. For the next several hours, they feasted on roasted corn, roasted bear meat, and countless other dishes, too many by far for Gabe to keep track of.

Then, when the feasting finally ended, the dancing began again.

This time Gabe and Annie stayed on the sidelines as spectators, their fingers intertwined.

CHAPTER NINE

Noises.

The sound of crockery rattling. The clang of a stove lid. Footsteps.

They woke Gabe who lay in his bed in Jackson Wolf's cabin. He stretched and listened to the sounds coming from the other part of the house and realized that Wolf must have come home from Ardmore.

He wanted to go back to sleep. The busk festival had lasted almost until dawn, and he was still sleepy. He yawned.

Gabe heard something fall to the floor and smash, followed by a muttered curse. He opened his eyes and then immediately closed them again against the bright yellow glare of the sun. Cautiously, he opened them again—but only part way. He squinted at the sun, then shaded his eyes.

Judging by the position of the sun in the sky, he decided it was well past noon. With a groan, he sat up and swung his legs over the side of the bed. Groggily, he reached for his clothes and began to dress. After pulling on his boots, he washed his face and hands, using the porcelain bowl and pitcher full of water that sat on top of the wooden dresser in the room. When he had finished his ablutions, he felt almost ready to face the world. He opened the door of his bedroom and went into the kitchen where he found Wolf frying eggs in a smoky skillet and boiling coffee.

"Morning," he said to the Lighthorseman who was swishing the eggs back and forth in the skillet.

"You look like you had a long night," Wolf commented.

"It *was* a long night."

"Was it a good one?"

"You bet. By the way, the Panthers won the game of toli."

"Hey, that's great!" Wolf exclaimed with a smile. "What was the score?"

Gabe told him and added, "In all modesty, I have to mention that I scored two points for our team."

"I knew you for a top-notch toli player the minute I first saw you."

Gabe went to the stove and poured himself a cup of coffee.

"Can you use some eggs?"

"Two."

Wolf slid two fried eggs with broken yolks onto a plate and placed them in front of his guest.

"What about Carmody? Did you find him?" Gabe asked.

"No, I didn't, dammit." Wolf fried himself two eggs and then sat down across from Gabe. "But he had been there, all right. I know that for sure because I went to the telegraph office and asked after him. The man on duty recognized the description of Carmody I gave him. I half-suspected that Dillworth had lied when he told us he sent Carmody to Ardmore to telegraph messages to Texas."

"What's the next move?"

"I'm heading out to the herd when I get finished here. I'll round up my men and try to see to it that the herd heads north this time."

"I'll go with you." Gabe paused a moment. "I don't reckon Dillworth's going to want to hand Carmody over to us. And, as far as Carmody's concerned, I don't think he'll go along with us without putting up a fight first."

"You're right on both scores, I suspect. You about ready to go?"

Gabe stuffed the last of the eggs he had been served into his mouth, washed them down with the last of the coffee in his cup, and rose. "Let's go."

They left the cabin and minutes later were leading their horses out of the barn. They swung into their saddles and rode out.

"We'll pick up reinforcements on the way," Wolf said.

But there was no one home at the first cabin they stopped at. At the next one, the wife of a Lighthorseman told Wolf that her husband and some other Lighthorsemen had ridden out earlier that morning after a man who had killed his neighbor with a hatchet following the busk festival and then fled the area.

"Looks like we're on our own," Wolf remarked as they left the cabin.

"Are there any federal marshals in the area that you know of?"

Wolf shook his head. "They drift in and out of the Nation. They work out of Fort Smith, Arkansas. We don't see a whole lot of them."

When Gabe said nothing, Wolf commented, "A hotshot toli player like you shouldn't be afraid to go up against that team of drovers led by Dillworth."

"Toli players don't tote guns."

"If you want to turn back—"

"I don't."

"I thought—"

"You were wrong."

The two men rode on in silence for several minutes.

"We won't stir things up when we get there," Wolf declared. "Maybe we can bluff them. Maybe they've already left and are on their way north."

"You're an optimist, I see."

"Not really. I suppose I'm just whistling in the dark."

"We could try the same maneuver as last time. Take a hostage."

"No, not this time. I'll just try to collect the money owed the Nation. Try to persuade Dillworth it's time he moved out. Try to take custody of Carmody."

"Us two up against the world."

"Maybe Lady Luck will smile on us."

Gabe hoped so.

He was still hoping so when he and Wolf arrived at Dillworth's cow camp.

The arrival of the two men halted the normal course of events in the vicinity. The men riding herd drew rein. The cook straightened up from his fire to stare at the new arrivals. Dillworth himself conspicuously placed his hand on the butt of the revolver hanging from his hip.

"What do you want?" he barked as Gabe and Wolf rode up to him.

"Same thing as before," Wolf answered, sounding businesslike. "We want you to pay the fees I told you about, and we want to take custody of Dave Carmody."

"Carmody's not here. He came back from Ardmore, but when I told him the police had been here hunting him, he lit a shuck."

"Where'd he go?" Gabe asked.

"How the hell should I know? I didn't ask the man about his travel plans."

Wolf's disappointment was etched on his face, but when he spoke his voice did not reflect it.

"Are you prepared to pay the fees?" he asked Dillworth.

"I'm afraid not," the trail boss replied almost nonchalantly.

"You mean to say that the cattle owners refused to ante up the money?" Gabe inquired.

"I mean," Dillworth drawled, "that I see no need to pay any fees of any kind, grazing or otherwise, under the circumstances."

"What circumstances are you talking about?" Wolf asked, his brow furrowing.

Dillworth removed a folded piece of paper from his vest pocket. He slowly unfolded it and then handed it to Wolf.

"Under the circumstances outlined in that telegraph message," he said in answer to the Lighthorseman's question.

Wolf took the paper and read it then handed it to Gabe who also read it.

"Now you know why I'm not about to pay any grazing fees or buy any permits of any kind or anything else of a like nature," Dillworth declared with smug satisfaction. "As you can plainly see, I've got permission to be on this land without handing over one red cent to any Indians."

Gabe read the telegraph message again, looking for some sort of loophole:

Per your request, permission is hereby granted for your men and animals to remain in your present location in Chickasaw Nation without paying any permit fees, fines, grazing fees, or any other charge imposed on you by that governmental body for the next ten days. To wit: until the seventeenth day of this month.
Signed: Percy McCullough, Secretary of the Interior

"You can't beat that card I played, can you, Wolf?" Dillworth taunted. "You know, I never sent Carmody to Ardmore to wire the cattle owners. I sent him there to wire some political friends of the cattle owners who I was told by the owners to contact if I ran into any kind of trouble on the trail north. Well, I did run into trouble—you, Wolf, and your policemen—and so I did what I'd been told to do. That telegram from Percy McCullough of the United States' government is the result. So why don't you and that other troublemaker you brought along with you turn right around and ride out of here and leave us be?"

"I'm not through with you yet, Mr. Dillworth," Wolf said. "I've got friends in high places, too, let me tell you."

"Well, why don't you just go talk to your friends in their high places and stop bothering me? I've got authorization to stay right where I am until the seventeenth, and that's exactly what I intend to do."

When Dillworth held out his hand, Gabe returned the telegraph message to him. Then, as the trail boss walked away, he and Wolf turned their mounts and rode out of the cow camp.

"That son of a bitch outfoxed us," Wolf muttered as they rode away together. "He's got more cards up his sleeve than a riverboat gambler, that man has."

"You said you had a high card or two up your sleeve, as I recall," Gabe reminded him. "What about these friends of yours in high places?"

"That was more bluff and bluster than anything else," Wolf reluctantly admitted. "I was thinking of a man named Lacey Graves."

"Who might he be?"

"He's a deputy to Chickasaw Nation who represents the Superintendent of the Five Civilized Tribes who is headquartered over in Muskogee in Creek Nation. I was thinking maybe Graves could set things straight for us so that we could collect the money due the tribal treasury or else move that herd off Chickasaw grazing land."

"We're going to call on him?"

"Might as well. But I don't really have very high hopes of accomplishing anything. Graves is little more than a lackey and a fairly spineless one at that."

"Where's he located?"

"Jimtown."

"Jimtown, here we come!"

They rode south then toward the Texas border, neither man saying much, both of them absorbed in their own thoughts. Gabe could sense Wolf's unhappiness with the way things had gone at the cow camp. The man was obviously feeling frustrated although he did not give voice to his feelings. But they were apparent in the stiff way he rode and in the tense expression on his face.

They were almost within sight of Jimtown when they saw the riders heading toward them.

"Aren't those fellows friends of yours?" Gabe asked Wolf as he recognized several familiar faces among the riders. The last time he had seen them they had been with Wolf during the Lighthorseman's first visit to Dillworth's cow camp.

"Hey, Warren!" Wolf called out and waved.

"We heard you were in Ardmore," the man named Warren said as he and the men with him drew rein and Wolf and Gabe did the same.

"I was. Who's that?"

Wolf pointed to the body slung facedown over the withers of Warren's blood bay.

"Arnie Randolph, that's who. He went berserk at the busk festival. He buried a hatchet in the head of Lenny Benson after some kind of argument they had. We caught up with him in Jimtown. He threw down on us—all of us. Would you believe that of old Arnie Randolph?"

"He was, as far as I knew, always a mild-mannered man."

"Well, he wasn't at the festival, I can tell you that. He turned into a wild man. As a result, Lenny Benson's dead and now so's Arnie. It was like he wanted us to shoot him. I never in all my born days heard of a man outgunned five to one drawing on those five. That's like committing suicide, that is. Where are you headed, Jackson?"

"Jimtown. Gabe and I—by the way, this is Gabe Conrad who's come over to our side. We went to Dillworth's cow camp today. We tried to apprehend Dave Carmody, the fellow that raped Annie Sadler. But Dillworth claimed he wasn't there. That he'd taken off for parts unknown."

"You sound like you don't believe what Dillworth told you."

"He could be lying. I wouldn't trust him as far as I could throw him. But I have to admit I saw no sign of Carmody."

"The last time I was out there with you, we couldn't find him hiding anywhere in the camp."

"Keep your eyes peeled for him. You have his description that Annie gave us. If you run into him, bring him in."

"We'll be on the scout for him, Jackson. You can count on that. Mind my asking what business you've got in Jimtown? Is it Lighthorsemen business?"

"It is, as a matter of fact. When we were at the cow camp,

I tried to get Dillworth to pay what he rightfully owes the tribal treasury, but he's a slick one. Seems he's gotten in touch with some powerful people in the government, and they saw to it that the Secretary of the Interior no less gave Dillworth permission to stay right where he is without having to pay Chickasaw Nation so much as a dime."

Warren whistled through his teeth and tilted his hat back on his head. "Dillworth swings a wide loop, it would appear."

"Gabe and I are heading to Jimtown to talk to Lacey Graves. Maybe he can get Dillworth to pay up or move out."

"Good luck to you," Warren called out as Wolf and Gabe resumed their journey.

Jimtown was a bustling settlement on the northern bank of the Red River and, like Red River Station, a haven for Texas renegades and shiftless drovers fired by their trail bosses on the way north. There was one church—on the edge of town—and eight saloons clustered in the center of town which, Gabe thought, said something about the town's priorities and value system.

He rode with Wolf down the rutted dirt rode that cut straight through the town from north to south, noting the absence of respectable women and the presence of their less reputable sisters, the soiled doves who leaned out of second story windows or loitered on street corners, their eyes never still and their lips making moves at the men passing by.

"There it is," Wolf said, pointing.

He had to repeat his words because Gabe's attention was fixed on a plump-hipped blond woman with breasts like ripe melons and shapely legs who was leaning against a lamp post, her arms folded in front of her, her blue eyes boring into his own.

"What?"

Wolf pointed to a first floor window in a wood frame building that bore the words in gold lettering: TRIBAL ADMINISTRATION.

Gabe guided his horse with his knees, turning toward the

building behind Wolf, his gaze still on the woman who was watching him with avid eyes as she provocatively licked her lips.

Both men dismounted and left their horses at the hitch rail in front of the building. Once inside, they found themselves confronting a pale-faced young man seated at a typewriting machine that rested ponderously on a desk behind which was a closed door.

The young man pushed his wire-rimmed spectacles up on his beak of a nose and squinted nearsightedly at Gabe and Wolf who were standing, hats in hands, in front of him. He reached up with one hand and patted his hair which was pomaded and parted in the middle.

"May I be of some service, gentlemen?" he said, his voice thin, almost a squeak.

"We're here to see Mr. Lacey Graves," Wolf told the man.

"Oh, dear, that is quite impossible at the present time," the man behind the desk declared. "Mr. Graves is engaged."

Gabe, annoyed at the man's supercilious and rather haughty manner, muttered, "We don't much care if he's married, let alone engaged. We mean to see him."

"But I thought I had made myself clear. Mr. Graves sees no one without an appointment." Another pat to the pomaded hair. "Do you have an appointment?"

"No," Wolf said, "but—"

"But," Gabe interrupted, "we got guns and we got knives and tempers that can turn a mouse like you into mincemeat in twenty seconds flat. Wolf, have you got your stopwatch?"

"Gabe," Wolf began in a conciliatory tone of voice.

"See here—" the man behind the desk began, leaning away from the two men on the far side of his small domain.

"*You* see here," Gabe barked. "Where's Graves?"

The man behind the desk swallowed hard and pointed to the door behind him.

"Let's go," Gabe said. He and Wolf rounded the desk and went through the door into the office beyond it.

"See here—" blustered the man seated behind a cherrywood desk that was dotted with several neat piles of precisely aligned papers.

"They've both caught the same damned disease—a bad case of 'see heres,' " Gabe said with a wink at Wolf.

"Mr. Graves, my name is Jackson Wolf. I'm a Lighthorseman. This is a friend and associate of mine, Mr. Gabe Conrad. We've come on tribal business."

"You can't come bursting in here—" Graves fell silent as Gabe's left hand ostentatiously fondled the butt of his revolver. "What is it you wish to discuss with me?" he asked.

"As you no doubt know," Wolf began, "Chickasaw Nation has been having difficulties with Texas cattlemen intruding on our territory without purchasing permits or paying per head grazing fees."

"Yes, yes, all that is nothing new."

"Well, sir," Wolf continued, "we've got a herd on the southern bank of the Washita River trail bossed by a man named Dillworth. Dillworth initially refused to pay the proper fees and then he enlisted the aid of some politically powerful people with the unhappy result that the United States' Secretary of the Interior has granted him the right to remain where he is for the time being without having to pay the fees rightly due Chickasaw Nation for the privilege of grazing his cattle on our land."

"Oh, my." Graves took a snuff box from his pocket, opened it, placed some snuff in one nostril, and sniffed delicately. "The Secretary of the Interior, you say?"

Wolf nodded.

Graves' eyes flicked from Wolf to Gabe's hand which remained on the butt of his revolver. "The Secretary has granted the herd permission to remain free of charge on Chickasaw land, you say?"

Wolf nodded again.

"Well, then"—Graves stuffed snuff into his other nostril—"I'm afraid there is really nothing I can do to help you in that case." A sniff.

"Nothing you can do?" Wolf repeated incredulously and glanced at Gabe.

"You represent the Superintendent of the Five Civilized

Tribes, as I understand it, here in Chickasaw Nation, is that right?" Gabe asked.

"That is correct."

"Then the way I see it, it's your job to enforce the laws on the books that—"

"See here—"

"There he goes again," Gabe said to Wolf with a sigh and a roll of his eyes.

"I cannot countermand an order issued by the Secretary of the Interior of the United States of America. That simply cannot be done. I have no such authority. Why, were I to do that, I would surely lose my position here. I would be dismissed for insubordination."

"Are you telling us," Wolf said, "that you're going to let Dillworth get away with what he's pulling?"

"The matter is out of my hands," Graves said with a certain smugness. "Now, if you gentlemen will excuse me, there are urgent matters demanding my immediate"—a meaningful pause—"and uninterrupted attention."

Gabe and Wolf stood there for a moment as Graves moved papers from one pile to another while ignoring them completely. Then they turned and left the office.

Once outside on the street, Wolf let loose a blistering oath. "I can't believe what just happened." He clapped his hat back on his head.

Gabe did the same. "It's like in a barnyard."

Wolf gave him a quizzical glance. "Chickens in a barnyard have what I've heard called a pecking order. Which means that one chicken pecks another and that one doesn't dare peck back but has to peck some other chicken which in turn—well, you get the picture. Same with politicians like Lacey Graves. He probably pecks that fellow he's got outside his office, but he's not about to peck back at the Secretary of the United States' Interior. He—"

Gabe stopped speaking and stared at the buxom blond he had noticed before entering Graves' office. She stared back.

"A fool's errand all right," Wolf was saying as he freed his reins from the hitch rail. "That's all this trip turned out to be."

"Maybe not altogether. You in a big hurry to head home?"

"No, I guess not. Why?"

Gabe pointed to the blond. "Maybe she's got a friend."

"Let's ask her," the Lighthorseman said with a smile.

They left their horses where they were and crossed the street to where the blond was standing, one hand on an upthrust hip.

"Howdy," Gabe greeted her. "How much?"

"You certainly don't beat about the bush, do you?" she remarked. "Two dollars."

"You know somebody who can service my friend here?"

The blond gave Wolf a professionally appraising look before responding. "Sure, I have. Lizzie is her name. She's in the hotel down the street. Room six. You knock on the door of room six for sex," she told Wolf with a giggle.

"I'm obliged to you, ma'am." He touched the brim of his hat to the blond and strode down the street, heading in a hurry for the hotel.

"I've got a place one street over," the woman said to Gabe.

They headed for it, making small talk along the way.

Once inside the blond's house, which was little more than a tar paper shack with newspapers lining the interior walls to keep the wind out, she held out a hand. "Two dollars. In advance."

"I wouldn't run out on you without paying."

The outstretched hand never wavered. "Some men have. So now I play it safe."

Gabe dug two dollars out of a pocket in his jeans and handed over the money. Minutes later they were both nude and lying side by side on the woman's bed.

"You got a name?" Gabe inquired as he nuzzled her neck.

"You can call me Dolly," the woman replied.

"I've got to get back to work," Dolly told Gabe as soon as they were done. She unceremoniously tossed his jeans and shirt to him.

He sat up and, like her, began to dress. She stood tapping her foot impatiently while she waited for him to finish, her own clothes already in place, and then preceeded him out of the house. He had to hurry to catch up with her.

When they reached the main street of town, she patted him on the cheek. "Look me up next time you're in the mood, honey." With that, she turned her attention to a short man who was striding along the boardwalk in her direction wearing a derby hat and spats.

As Gabe left her, he heard Dolly say, "Looking for a good time, mister?"

Apparently, the man was because they were on their way to Dolly's domicile within seconds, she holding tightly to his arm and he staring lustfully at her cleavage which was about level with his nose.

Gabe crossed the street and untied his and Wolf's horses. He led them next door to where a wooden water trough stood and let them drink. Before they could take in too much water, he jerked their heads up and led them back to the hitch rail. He leaned against it idly and watched Jimtown's passing parade of people, mostly hard cases who looked like border bandits mixed in with a sprinkling of Texas trash clearly identifiable by their drawls.

Wolf joined him a few minutes later. "How was it?" he asked.

"Fine and dandy. How about you?"

Wolf let his smile say it all.

As they boarded their horses and rode out of Jimtown, Gabe said, "I watered the horses. But I didn't let them drink too much since we've got a way to go."

Wolf nodded approvingly.

By the time they arrived back at Wolf's home that evening, they were both hungry. After they had seen to their horses, Wolf began to prepare supper. But, before he could serve it or even get it well under way, there was a knock on his door. Gabe got up from the kitchen table and opened it.

"Jackson here?" asked the man named Warren who had

been with the other Lighthorsemen Gabe and Wolf had met while on their way south to Jimtown.

"He's here. Come in."

"What's up, Warren?" Wolf asked when he saw who his visitor was.

"Got some good news for you, Jackson."

"I could use some."

"We got him."

"Who? Hey, are you talking about Dave Carmody?"

"The very same."

"Where'd you find him?" Wolf asked, abandoning his skillet and spatula.

"We were passing the Dillworth herd on the bank of the Washita River on our way home after running into you and Gabe, and there he was riding herd. We rode up and before he knew what had hit him, we had taken him into custody."

"You had no trouble?"

"Oh, Dillworth did his little dance and told us we were arresting an innocent man. One of the drovers pulled a gun on us. I don't think he'll be much good to Dillworth for a while. I put a bullet in his right leg which made him decide real quick that he didn't want to hang onto his gun any longer. Made the other drovers gun-shy as well."

"Where have you got Carmody?" Gabe inquired.

"He's under guard down in the glade right this minute. We've got a bullwhip all oiled up, and we're ready to make him regret the day he ever touched Annie Sadler. But the boys thought you'd want to be there to watch the proceedings so I came on over here to fetch you."

"Let's go," Wolf said, heading for the door. But then he stopped. "You want to stay and cook yourself something to eat, Gabe? You could join us later if that suits your fancy."

"I'll go with you now. Supper can wait. I want to see how you Chickasaws mete out justice."

"Come on then."

Gabe followed the two Lighthorsemen out of the cabin and soon the three of them were heading at a brisk walk for the glade where the busk festival had been held.

When they arrived, they found Dave Carmody seated cross-legged on the ground, being guarded by two armed Lighthorsemen. Also present among the Chickasaws gathered in the glade were Annie Sadler and her grandfather. Annie stood with her eyes averted from Carmody, but her grandfather was glaring at him, his fists clenched at his sides. A Chickasaw man whom Gabe had never seen before stood nearby with a black leather bullwhip coiled in his hand.

"Let's get on with it," Warren called out to Carmody's guards who immediately responded by jerking Carmody to his feet and marching him toward a tall post oak.

"Wait!" the vainly struggling Carmody yelled. "You can't do this! You've got no proof that I did what she claimed. She's lying!" He managed to point an accusing finger at Annie who flinched as if he had threatened her.

"We've been through all that, Carmody," Warren declared. "Annie pointed you out as the man who raped her."

"It's her word against mine!" Carmody argued, still struggling to free himself from his guards. "And I say I didn't do it!"

"Let him go!"

Everyone in the glade turned toward the spot where the words had come from.

Dillworth, gun in hand, stood there. "My men have surrounded this place," he told the throng. "If anybody makes a false move, he dies."

As if Dillworth's words had been a signal, his drovers emerged from the shelter of the trees, all of them armed, some of them with more than one gun, to confront the gathered Chickasaws that they had encircled.

"Let him go," Dillworth repeated.

"Boss, I sure as hell am glad to see you!" Carmody exclaimed, breaking into a grin. "These savages were going to whip me."

The two guards released Carmody, and he hurried over to stand beside Dillworth who announced, "We followed the trail you policemen left to get here. Now we're heading back to our camp on the Washita. If anybody tries to follow us, we'll shoot to kill."

"No!" The word had been shouted by Annie Sadler.

She left her grandfather's side and stepped out into the center of the glade. Shaking a fist at Dillworth, she cried, "You can't take him. He has to be punished for what he did to me!"

"I don't know for a fact that he did anything to you," Dillworth responded coldly.

"He did!" Annie then passionately and eloquently described her rape at the hands of Carmody. "I am not lying," she concluded. "I have no reason to lie about what happened."

Sadler walked across the glade toward Dillworth, apparently unconcerned about Dillworth's gun or what the trail boss might do with it.

"My granddaughter is not lying," he said. "She is telling the truth. You can take your man away from us, but we will not rest until justice—Chickasaw justice—has been done to him."

"Boss, you're not going to listen to them, are you?" Carmody asked uneasily.

"Who are you?" Dillworth asked Sadler.

"I am Harley Sadler. Once upon a far better time I was the Principal Chief of the Chickasaw tribe. I am the grandfather of the woman that man"—he indicated Carmody—"raped so brutally."

"Don't pay him no mind, Boss," Carmody pleaded. "The man's a drunk. I saw him the night he claims I raped his granddaughter in that Chickasaw saloon up on the hill back there. He was cadging money for booze from the people in the place."

"Is that true?" Dillworth asked.

Sadler hesitated.

Dillworth repeated his question.

Reluctantly, almost inaudibly, Sadler admitted, "Yes, it's true." Then, defiantly, he said, "I had no money. I was trying to borrow money from my friends so I could buy a drink. What's wrong with a man needing money? That's got nothing at all to do with what happened to my grand-daughter."

Gabe saw Annie turn her back to her grandfather in evident shame. He also saw the crafty expression that spread across Dillworth's face as he stared thoughtfully at Sadler. He could not hear the rest of the conversation that took place between Dillworth and Sadler, but he could not help hearing Dillworth's subsequent loud remarks directed to the assembled Chickasaws.

"Take Carmody," the trail boss said to them, "and do what you've been intending to do to him. Me and my men won't attempt to stop you."

Gabe stared in disbelief as Dillworth gestured to his men, indicating that they were to leave the area, and then walked away himself with his arm around Harley Sadler's shoulder. He watched the pair until they were out of sight and then turned back to watch the guards drag a vociferously protesting Carmody to a post oak tree.

"Goddamn you, Dillworth!" Carmody roared. "You've gone and sold me down the river, damn you! Well, you've not heard the end of this matter, you bastard! I'll even up the score between you and me before long! You'll see! I will!"

The guards wrapped Carmody's arms around the trunk of the tree and tied his hands behind it so that his chest was pressed tightly up against the oak's rough bark. One of them ripped Carmody's shirt to bare his back. The other guard signaled, and the man with the bullwhip moved toward the tree at a steady, almost stately, pace.

When he was with a few yards of it, he halted and uncoiled his whip. Spreading his feet to steady himself, he raised his whip and then lashed out with it.

Carmody's body jerked as the black leather struck his bare back. The next time the whip bit into his exposed flesh his head jerked backward. The third time the whip landed on his back, he let out a yell.

As the whipping continued, Carmody began to scream uncontrollably.

Gabe found himself counting the lashes. Six, seven . . .

. . . nineteen, twenty. It was over. The man who had carried out Carmody's punishment walked away, trailing his bloodied whip.

The guards untied Carmody who slumped to the ground, his cheek pressed against the trunk of the tree, his eyes closed. Blood ran in bright red rivulets from the open wounds crisscrossing his back.

Gabe glanced at Annie. She was standing not far away from him, an expression of utter satisfaction on her face.

CHAPTER TEN

The next morning after breakfast with Wolf, Gabe leaned back in his chair and commented, "We've solved one problem. But one still remains."

"I take it you're talking, in the first instance, about Dave Carmody." When Gabe nodded, Wolf continued. "He left last night with his tail between his legs which I suppose any man who endured the whipping he did would have done. As for the other problem you mentioned, I assume you mean the continued presence of the Dillworth herd on the Washita."

"Have you given any thought to telegraphing the Superintendent of the Five Civilized Tribes about the problem?"

"As a matter of fact, I have. In fact, I've done more than merely given the matter some thought. I took action. I sent Warren up to Ardmore to telegraph the superintendent. I asked for permission to move the herd out of the Nation."

"Do you think you'll get it?"

"That's hard to say. On the one hand, the superintendent generally acts on behalf of the Nation in disputes of this kind. He's a fair man and not unaware of the problems we've been having of late with intruding Texas cattlemen. On the other hand, he may not want to go against his own deputy in this matter. He might consider such a move bad politics. We'll just have to wait and see."

"If it turns out that he does back you up, what then?"

"We'll ride out—all the Lighthorsemen I can round up—and take a stand." Wolf filled the bowl of a clay pipe with tobacco and tamped it down. He struck a match, lit his pipe, and sat there smoking while Gabe finished the last of his coffee which had begun to cool.

Wolf was still smoking some time later, his head wreathed in a gray cloud, when there was a knock on the door. He rose and opened the door to find Warren standing outside.

"Here's your answer," the Lighthorseman told Wolf and handed him a piece of paper.

Wolf ushered Warren into the room, put down his pipe, and read the telegraph message he had just been given. When he looked up from it, there was a broad smile on his face.

"Well, Gabe, it looks like we're one up on Dillworth," he crowed.

"The superintendent wants him and his herd out of the Nation?"

"Immediately, according to his message. 'Without delay,' to put it in his words." Wolf looked down at the paper in his hand. "He says, and I quote: 'If Dillworth makes delay or causes the Lighthorsemen any undue difficulty, let me know immediately, and federal marshals will be sent to the area at once.' I don't think Dillworth will like that last part much, do you?"

"When are we going to show him that?" Warren asked, indicating the telegraph message in Wolf's hand.

"We'll ride out there now. We can pick up the rest of our men—as many as are available—on our way."

Gabe rose and followed the two Chickasaws out of the cabin into the morning's bright sunlight.

When he and Wolf had gotten their horses ready to ride, both men rode out with Warren. On the way to the Washita River, they stopped at other Chickasaw dwellings, and by the time the river came into view, they were a party of ten—nine Lighthorsemen and Gabe.

"We'd better be ready for some shooting," Gabe said as they galloped along. "You heard what Dillworth said before when he had us all under his and his men's guns."

"He said he'd shoot us if we followed him," Wolf recalled. "But you know there's a funny thing about that. He said it when he had the drop on us, but he didn't say it when he finally did leave after his little private talk with Harley Sadler last night."

"Come to think of it, you're right," Warren mused. "Maybe he had himself a change of heart. Maybe the man's turned kindly toward us."

"Don't bet on it," Wolf cautioned.

Later, when they came within sight of the river, Wolf said, "Get your guns out, boys, and be ready for anything."

They rode slowly into the cow camp, their eyes roving from side to side, the guns in their hands cocked and ready for action.

But no one fired at them. Surprisingly, most of the drovers ignored them as they continued attending to their chores. A few men did watch their approach, and their faces wore no hostile expressions but rather ones that might be interpreted as mild amusement. Dillworth waved a welcome to them.

"Something's not right," Warren muttered. "The way they're acting's not natural. I thought for sure they would have tried to blow us to hell by now."

"Keep your eyes peeled," Wolf cautioned.

Gabe said nothing as he silently speculated on the reason for the strange behavior of Dillworth and his drovers.

He and the Lighthorsemen drew rein in front of Dillworth but stayed in their saddles.

"Nice day," Dillworth remarked. "Might rain though. See those clouds off there to the south? They're rain clouds or I miss my guess."

Small talk about the weather from a man who had threatened to shoot to kill anybody who followed him and his men when they left the glade where Carmody was whipped? It made no sense to Gabe. Worse, it worried him. When snakes smile at you, he thought to himself, that's the time to take cover.

"I guess you know why I've come," Wolf said.

"I guess I do," Dillworth said offhandedly.

"I've got a telegraph message here from the Superintendent of the Five Civilized Tribes who, as you may or may
not know, makes the rules and regulations for Chickasaw
Nation under the combined authority of the tribal and United States' governments."

"I'd heard something to that effect."

"Read it." Wolf handed Dillworth the telegraph message.

Dillworth took it from him and read it. He handed it
back.

"Well?" Wolf prompted.

"Well what?"

"You read what the superintendent had to say. It's time
for you and your herd to make tracks."

"We're staying."

"Dillworth, you're lookin for trouble," Wolf warned,
"when you take it upon yourself to ignore an order from the
superintendent. You read what he said in that message about
sending a swarm of federal marshals down here if you get
your back up and refuse to budge. Is that what you want?"

"I don't think you fellows fully understand the situation,"
Dillworth said almost amiably. "Maybe that's because you
don't keep yourself current. This is a fast-moving world we
live in, Mr. Lighthorseman. Your newfound friend there,
Gabe Conrad, found that out recently. One minute he's
working for me; the next minute he's fired and right back
to being just another saddle tramp."

"Dillworth, I don't know what the hell you're talking
about," an exasperated Wolf exclaimed.

"Then I'll tell you what I'm talking about." The trail
boss' tone was no longer amiable. It had turned firm. His
eyes had turned from mild to stony. "I also have a piece of
paper to put up against that telegraph message of yours."

Dillworth took his time about removing the piece of
paper from his vest pocket. He handed it up to Wolf who
took it, read it, and muttered, "Well, I'll be damned!"

"What's it say?" Gabe asked.

Wolf handed the paper to him.

Gabe saw at once that the paper he held in his hand was nothing more nor less than a bill of sale. It stated that Dillworth had sold his entire herd of cattle for "a mutually agreed upon sum" to none other than Harley Sadler, the former Principal Chief of the Chickasaw tribe. It was signed by both Sadler and Dillworth.

"That paper sort of puts our little dispute in a brand new light, now doesn't it, Mr. Lighthorseman?" Dillworth crowed.

"I don't get it, Dillworth," Gabe said before Wolf could respond to Dillworth's taunt. "Why the hell would you sell your cows to Sadler?"

"That's an easy question to answer," Dillworth replied. "But let's start back at the beginning of this matter which happens to be when Sadler and I first met. That was, you'll recollect, when you Chickasaws were fixing to whip the hide off Dave Carmody.

"Maybe you remember that Carmody told me he'd seen Sadler in the local Chickasaw saloon cadging drinks. Then Sadler admitted to me that what Carmody had said was the truth when I asked him if it was. That's when I got the inkling of an idea. Sadler clinched it for me when he indicated to me that he was in need of money. All at once, I saw a way out of the dilemma I was in over grazing rights. I had till the seventeenth to stay where I was thanks to the Secretary of the Interior. But I wasn't sure that would be enough time to turn the trick for me. Those beeves of mine keep eating, but so far they're not much fatter than they were when we first got here to the Washita.

"What I needed, I had already decided, was another high card I could play in order to stay put as long as necessary. But I didn't see any in the deck I was holding. I didn't, that is, until Harley Sadler, ex-Chickasaw chief and present drunk, turned up to help me solve the problem I was facing."

"You bribed him," Wolf muttered. "You gave him money to sign that bill of sale. How much did you give him, Dillworth?"

"Thirty dollars."

"Wait a minute," Gabe said. "I still don't get it. Why in the world," he asked Wolf, "would Dillworth sign over his herd to Sadler and pay him thirty dollars to take it off his hands? It doesn't make sense to me. No way does it."

"I'll wager your Mr. Lighthorseman there can explain it to you," Dillworth told Gabe, jerking a thumb in Wolf's direction.

"I think I know what happened," Wolf said. "You saw Dillworth take Sadler aside. Well, he must have offered Sadler money—thirty dollars—to sign a bill of sale and become the nominal owner of the cattle. But, in fact, that bill of sale isn't worth the paper it's written on.

"Because Sadler doesn't really own the cattle. Dillworth has set things up so that legally it appears that Sadler owns the herd. But if Sadler were ever to try to take possession of the herd—which I'm sure he's not interested in doing— I'd bet my bottom dollar that Dillworth would probably put a bullet in his brain. Am I right, Dillworth?"

"Right on the money! When I made Sadler my offer, he jumped at it. He wanted booze so bad he not only would have signed the bill of sale I wrote out, he would have gotten down on his knees and licked my boots if I'd told him that he had to do that as part of the bargain. The man's a shameless degenerate. All he cares about is getting drunk. Of course, it takes money to get drunk. I supplied the money he needed."

Wolf glanced at Gabe and said, "He's done it. Dillworth's got us over a barrel. As long as he's got that bill of sale that says Harley Sadler owns the herd, there is no way we can make him move those cows off this land. You see, Chickasaw land is owned in common by all the members of the tribe, each of whom can, within reason, use it for any purpose he wishes. What we have here then, as a direct result of the bribe Dillworth paid to Sadler, is Chickasaw cattle grazing on Chickasaw land."

"You're saying the cattle can't be forced off the land because a member of the tribe supposedly owns them."

"That's it," Wolf said sorrowfully.

Dillworth began to laugh, holding his sides and rocking back and forth on his boot heels. When his laughter subsided a few minutes later, he said mockingly, "I work for Harley Sadler now, Mr. Lighthorseman. Those cattle you see spread out down there by the river, they're his now as a result of the arrangement I made with him. You don't happen to have any plans to try to run Chickasaw cattle off Chickasaw land, now do you?"

The trail boss' laughter followed Wolf, Gabe, Warren, and the others as they turned their horses and rode away from the cow camp.

Once they were out of sight of Dillworth and his drovers, Gabe held up a hand to call a halt. "I've got an idea. If what I've got in mind pans out, maybe we can still move Dillworth and his cows off that land back there and out of Chickasaw Nation altogether. I've got some riding to do. You boys stay put right here till I get back. Will you do that?"

"How long before you get back?" Wolf inquired.

"Not long. And if things work out the way I hope they will, we'll have Dillworth in a box he can't get out of."

"We know now," Warren mused, "why he didn't repeat his threat of shooting to kill if anybody followed him when he finally did take his leave after talking to Sadler. He had no need to threaten us since he'd just struck his deal with Sadler. He could welcome us with open arms just the way he did when we arrived back there because he knew he had us by the balls, having gotten Sadler to sign that bill of sale."

Gabe nodded and then left the Lighthorsemen, heading north.

When he arrived at his destination, everything was quiet. No sound came from the cabin as he dismounted and left his horse ground-hitched in front of it. No smoke rose from the cabin's stone chimney. No one answered the door when he knocked on it.

He gripped the latch and pulled the door open. It creaked on its iron hinges, the sound still the only one anywhere in the area of the cabin. He peered into the gloomy interior of the building. At first, he saw no one and heard nothing. But then he heard a click. Soft. So soft he almost doubted that he had really heard it. Then—another click. As his eyes became accustomed to the gloom inside the cabin, he was able to make out a figure seated in a rocking chair in front of the cold hearth.

"Click. Click-click." The sound of the rocker striking the stone flags that formed the hearth.

"Annie?"

Annie Sadler continued rocking slowly, rhythmically, as she stared into the cold hearth. She did not turn her head or in any other way acknowledge Gabe's presence in the home she shared with her grandfather.

"Annie, are you alright?" he asked, moving closer and taking up a position between her and the fireplace.

She looked up at him, and he was chilled by the depth of sorrow he saw swimming in her black eyes. He watched two tears slide slowly down her cheeks.

"He's dead," she said dully.

"Who's dead?"

"My Grandpapa."

Gabe was taken aback by the news. "What happened to him?"

"He's in the barn."

When Annie said no more, not even when he asked a second time about what had happened to Sadler, Gabe rose and left the cabin. In the barn, he stood staring at the body dangling from a hemp rope that had been tied to one of the barn's beams high overhead. He must've jumped down from the hayloft, Gabe thought, as Sadler's corpse, its broken neck bent at a forty-five degree angle, slowly turned first one way, then the other. Sadler's eyes bulged sightlessly. His tongue was thrust between his teeth and had turned purple.

Gabe returned to the cabin.

"Annie, I'm sorry."

"So am I. But at least he's at peace now." She bent forward, buried her face in her hands and began to sob.

"It's my fault," she wailed through her trembling fingers. "It's all my fault."

Gabe went and hunkered down in front of her. Gently, he took her hands away from her tear-stained face. "What happened? Can you tell me?"

Annie choked back a sob. She used both hands to wipe the tears from her tawny cheeks.

"I slept late this morning. I had been awake most of last night. I couldn't sleep. I kept seeing that man—Carmody. I kept hearing the sound of the whip as it whistled through the air and landed on his bare back. I didn't fall asleep until dawn.

"When I awoke, I heard Grandpapa in the kitchen. He was singing an old Chickasaw warrior's song. I dressed and went out to him. He was thumping the table with the heels of his hands as if it were a drum. He was drunk."

Annie swallowed hard and began biting her lower lip.

"Can you go on?"

She hesitated and then nodded. "Something inside me seemed to snap. I became angry. Angrier than I can recall being in my entire life. There he was again, I thought, sniveling and singing and making a spectacle of himself. He stank of whiskey.

"I screamed at him. I called him names. Terrible names. Names I had never spoken aloud before. I cursed him. I said he was ruining my life. Finally, I said I hated him enough to kill him."

"What did he say?"

"Nothing. He stopped singing. He stared at me. Then he gave a sad little sigh. He began to weep. The tears rolled out of his eyes and down his cheeks."

"Then what happened?"

"He turned and slowly corked the bottle of whiskey that was on the table in front of him. He wiped his hands on his trousers as if they had became dirty from touching the bottle. He stood up. It was then that he said, 'You're right, my dear granddaughter. Everything you said about me just now is true. The names you called me—they all fit, I am ashamed to say.'

"His voice was suprisingly steady as he spoke. He didn't slur his words as he had been doing while singing. He sat down again. He asked me for a piece of paper and a pencil. I gave them to him. He began to write something. When he had finished, he looked up at me and said, 'I saw what happened.'"

Gabe frowned. "What did he mean?"

"He meant that he had seen—what happened to me that night when Dave Carmody came here."

"But he never said anything before, did he?" When Annie shook her head, Gabe asked, "Why do you think he admitted it now and why didn't he do anything to help you that night?"

"I gather what I had just said to him made him realize how low he had sunk. So he confessed to having witnessed the attack. I know for certain that he had never said anything about being a witness to the rape before because he told me himself before he went out to the barn and hanged himself that he had been too drunk that night to come to my aid. He said he had seen what was happening through the window. He said he tried to come to my aid but simply couldn't. He couldn't get up from his bed. He was too drunk, in his own words, to do anything other than helplessly watch."

Annie's words chilled Gabe. He said nothing, but his thoughts raced.

"I should never have said to him what I did," Annie continued. "If I hadn't, if I had been more understanding, he'd be alive now."

"You have every right in the world to speak your mind. You also had every right to let your grandpa know how you felt about what he was doing to you and to himself."

"But—"

"All you did was tell him the truth."

Annie considered what Gabe had said, her intertwined fingers twisting in her lap. "It could be said then, if you're right, that the truth killed him."

"I am right and, yes, that's about the size of it, as I see it. The truth killed him. You didn't."

Annie stopped rocking and looked up at Gabe. "That paper I mentioned—the one Grandpapa wrote on."

"What about it?"

She reached into the pocket of the apron she was wearing and removed a piece of paper which she offered to Gabe. "You'll want this."

He took the paper from her, unfolded it, and read what was written on it. "Thank you," he said when he had finished. "I do want this. It will help Jackson Wolf and his men clear that herd of cattle out of Chickasaw Nation."

"I'm afraid what's written there doesn't mean anything to me."

"Your grandpa says here"—Gabe held up the paper—"that the deal he made with Dillworth, the trail boss of the herd down on the Washita, is fraudulent. Dillworth paid your grandpa thirty dollars to make that deal."

"Thirty dollars," Annie repeated thoughtfully. "I wondered where Grandpapa got the money to buy the whiskey he was drinking when I got up this morning."

"He got it from Dillworth like I said. Dillworth signed his cattle over to your grandpa so that he could legally keep them on Chickasaw land since the bill of sale says a Chickasaw owns them. It was a sneaky deal to keep Wolf from running Dillworth off tribal land until Dillworth was good and ready to go."

"Apparently he regretted his action. He repudiates the so-called sale in that note he left."

"I came here to try to talk him into doing that very thing."

"Thirty pieces of silver," Annie murmured.

"Beg pardon?"

"In the Christian Bible, I have read where Judas Iscariot betrayed Jesus Christ for thirty pieces of silver. My Grandpapa betrayed his people by the deal he made with Dillworth for thirty dollars."

"I know this is none of my business, Annie, but what do you plan to do now that your grandpa's gone?"

"After I bury him, I'm going to leave here. I'm not sure where I'm going. It will be far from here where no one knows me. Someplace where I can start a new life where no one knows I've been raped."

"You'll do fine, I know you will. You're a strong and loving woman. Those are two traits that'll see you through any stormy weather you run into in the days and years yet to come."

"We're saying good-bye, aren't we, Gabe?"

"I reckon we are."

Annie bent over and placed a chaste kiss on Gabe's cheek.

She said nothing, and he knew there was nothing more he could say. He stood up, gently touched her cheek and then turned and left the cabin.

Gabe rejoined Wolf and the other Lighthorsemen less than an hour later. As he brought his galloping buckskin to a halt, he slid down to the ground and wordlessly handed Sadler's suicide note to Wolf.

The Lighthorseman took it from him and read it. When he had finished doing so, he let out a wild whoop of delight and handed the note to Warren.

Minutes later, all the Lighthorsemen were congratulating one another and telling one another that now they had the means to move Dillworth's herd out of Chickasaw Nation once and for all.

"Hold on," Gabe told them. "You're forgetting one important thing."

The noisy banter died down as all the men stared, puzzled, at Gabe.

"Even with Sadler's note repudiating the sale of the cattle to him, Dillworth's still got permission from the Secretary of the Interior to remain right where he is until the seventeenth of this month. Unless I miss my guess, he'll set things up so that by the end of that time he'll have managed to have gotten himself an extension of that time period."

Glum expressions settled on the faces of the Lighthorsemen as Wolf muttered, "I'd forgotten all about that telegraph message in the excitement of the moment."

A vague memory stirred in Gabe's mind. A memory having something to do with the telegraph message. But he couldn't quite recall what it was. He tried his best but, for the life of him, he couldn't dredge up the memory that was now gnawing at him.

"We might as well all go home," Warren suggested. "There's not much point to taking this note Sadler left to Dillworth and showing it to him. He'll just pull out that telegraph message of his that says he can stay right where he's at until the seventeenth of this month."

Warren's words did it. They dislodged the mental block in Gabe's mind and triggered his memory of the precise words of the Secretary of the Interior's telegram, the ones which said, he now recalled: " . . . permission is hereby granted for your men and animals to remain in your present location . . ." It was Gabe's turn to let out a wild whoop.

"What is it, Gabe?" Wolf asked.

"You think of a way to beat Dillworth?" Warren asked.

"I think I have. Now, listen up. Here's what we're going to do."

Minutes later, all the men were mounted and riding hard toward Dillworth's cow camp.

But before they reached it or could even see it, they heard the sound of gunfire coming from its direction.

Gabe and Wolf exchanged glances, but neither man said anything. Not until they topped a rise and could see the camp in the distance.

Then Gabe said, "Carmody."

"Looks like he's made good on his threat to get even with Dillworth for letting him be bull-whipped," Wolf said as he sat his saddle watching the furious gunfight taking place down below. "Where'd he get those three men with him?"

"Maybe we should just stay here and let them all kill each other," Warren suggested, half-seriously. "That'd solve our problem for sure."

"We'll break it up," Gabe said. "Then we'll do what we came here to do. Wolf, take a few men and come in on Carmody's left flank. Warren you and the rest move in on Carmody from their right flank."

"What are you going to do, Gabe?" Warren inquired.

"I'm going to join Dillworth and his drovers. See if I can't help him send Carmody and his bad boys packing—with the help of all of you fellows, of course."

"Well, that's a twist," Wolf said with a ghost of a smile. "I never thought I'd see the day when you'd be siding with a sworn enemy."

"Dillworth's not my sworn enemy," Gabe said. "Where'd you ever get that idea?" He smiled. "He's more a pain in the ass I'm anxious to get rid of any which way I can."

When the two groups of Lighthorsemen had gone their separate ways, Gabe circled in a wide arc around the gun-fight until he was some distance behind Dillworth and his drovers. Then he dismounted, leaving his horse ground-hitched, and moved up to join them.

When he reached the chuck wagon where Dillworth had taken cover, he hoisted down the half-full water barrel and, hunkering down, took up a defensive position behind it. As he fired his first shot at the men attacking the cow camp, a startled Dillworth glanced over his shoulder and saw him. "What the hell are you doing here?" Dillworth yelled.

"Came to join the party even if I wasn't invited." Gabe's second shot clipped one of the attackers in the right bicep, forcing a yelp of pain from the wounded man.

"The hell you say," Dillworth muttered, suspicion bright in his eyes. "You're not here to do me any good, I'll bank on that."

"They say," Gabe began as he squinted and took aim at Carmody, "you shouldn't look a gift horse in the mouth." He squeezed off a shot but missed his target. The round did however force Carmody down behind a boulder.

But less than a minute later, Carmody's head and gun appeared and flame flashed from his weapon's barrel as he fired at Curly who was prone on the ground, both hands gripping the butt of his revolver. Carmody's shot was high and went over Curly's head.

"Who the hell are they?" Dillworth spluttered as Wolf, Warren, and the rest of the Lighthorsemen moved in on the flanks of the attackers, their guns blazing. "Aren't they—"

"You recognize some of them, do you? They're Chicka-saw police come to help save the day for you."

"Are you mocking me, Conrad?"

Gabe didn't bother to reply. He fired another round. Before the smoke from the barrel of his gun had dissipated, he fired again.

"You scored a hit," Dillworth exulted as one of the attackers stood up, clutched his chest with both hands where blood was blossoming, spun around, and fell face down on the ground.

The Lighthorsemen had halted their advance and taken cover, but they continued to fire upon Carmody and the men with him.

Gabe was close enough to Carmody to hear the man's curses. He watched Carmody fire first to the right, then to the left, then turn to face the drovers and fire yet again.

"Carmody's outgunned and he knows it," Gabe told Dillworth. "What's more he's nervous. He's shooting at spooks half the time. Men he can't see. I say we charge him and his men."

"A frontal attack?" a skeptical Dillworth asked. "Are you out of your mind?"

"I don't think so. But if you're too timid to try that, I'll do it myself."

"You'll what?"

Gabe rose from behind the water barrel. Waving his free hand above his head, he gestured to the Lighthorsemen. His unmistakable signal for them to move in on their foes galvanized the Chickasaws into action. They rose up on both flanks of Carmody's position and went racing toward the men attacking the cow camp.

At the same instant, Gabe rounded the chuck wagon and sprinted toward the attackers.

As the three-pronged assault continued, one of the men with Carmody leaped to his feet and yelled, "Don't shoot! I surrender!"

"Get down, goodamn you!" Carmody yelled at the man who ignored him as he stood weaponless with both hands pointing at the sky.

A second man also rose, dropped his revolver, and raised his hands.

The Lighthorsemen were within yards of their position now. So was Gabe.

Carmody leaped up and began firing wildly. His fire was returned. Suddenly he went flying backward to the right, dropping his gun and grabbing his chest. He lay still where he landed, blood soaking his shirt.

Gabe came to a halt not far from the body. As the Lighthorsemen joined him, he ejected spent shells from the cylinder of his gun and calmly replaced them with rounds he had thumbed out of his cartridge belt.

"Two dead, two survivors," Wolf commented, looking around the battlefield. "Carmody didn't make it. Who shot him, do you know?"

"Someone on his left flank," Gabe said. "Not that it matters."

"What are we going to do with those two?" Warren asked, pointing at the two men with their hands still in the air.

"Don't shoot us!" one of them pleaded, his eyes wide with fear.

"How'd you fellows get hooked up with Carmody?" Wolf asked.

"We ran into him down in Red River. He hired us to side him. Said he had a grudge to settle with the boss of that there cow camp."

"Shoot them both." The words were spoken by Dillworth as he walked up to stand beside Wolf.

"No more killing," Gabe said sharply. "The fight's over."

"You're going to let those two just walk away?" an incredulous Dillworth inquired.

"On your way," Gabe told the two men.

They looked at him skeptically for a moment. "You're not going to shoot us in the back when we turn around, are you?" one of them asked.

"I'm no back-shooter," Gabe said.

"What about him?" One of the men indicated Dillworth with a nod of his head.

"He won't shoot you," Gabe promised. "Now, get on your horses and get out of here."

The men slowly lowered their hands and began to back away toward where four horses stood. When they reached them, they climbed into their saddles and, leading the other two horses, galloped away and out of sight.

"We should have shot them," Dillworth grumbled. Then, glancing at Gabe, he said, "I like the way you men came to my aid, though I still can't help wondering why you did it."

"You may like what we just did," Gabe said laconically, "but I don't think you're going to like what we're about to do."

"What are you talking about?" Dillworth asked uneasily, his eyes narrowing.

"Get their guns," Gabe ordered.

When the Lighthorsemen had disarmed Dillworth and his drovers, Gabe said, "Let's do it. Let's do it *now,* men!"

Gabe sprinted toward his horse, leaped onto it, and went galloping away with the Lighthorsemen as the startled Dillworth and his dismayed drovers stared after them. They headed for the herd that was peacefully grazing along the southern bank of the Washita River.

Working skillfully together, the men spread out in a long line paralleling the herd. Then, on a signal from Gabe, they turned their horses sharply to the right and went galloping toward the herd.

At the sound of the horse's pounding hooves, some of the cattle raised their heads and stared nervously at the approaching line of riders. Others began to move away from them toward the river. Most of them began to low. One or two, more frightened than the rest, began to bawl. Within minutes, they were almost all in the water. A few head had begun to race along the bank, seeking to escape the men who now were shouting at the top of their voices and waving coiled ropes or slickers as they rode.

The strays were quickly cut off and sent splashing into the water. Soon the entire herd was in the water and so were the riders who were forcing the cattle to cross to the northern bank of the river.

The cattle emerged dripping from the water and they climbed up onto the river bank, followed by their pursuers.

"Here they come!" Warren yelled. He pointed at Dillworth and his drovers who were on their horses and riding through the river. "And they sure don't look like the happiest of men!" he added.

Gabe and the others drew rein and waited for Dillworth and his men to arrive. When they did, they were shouting questions. Their voices drowned each other out as the irate cattlemen all talked and shouted at once.

Gabe held up a hand. He waited until they had fallen silent. Then he produced Sadler's suicide note and handed it to Dillworth.

The trail boss read it and then looked up at Gabe. "So?"

"So those cattle belong to you, not Harley Sadler. Sadler's reneged on your deal."

"So?" Dillworth repeated.

"So it's time you moved them out of Chickasaw Nation," Gabe declared.

Dillworth muttered an oath. "Are we going to do that dumb dance again?" Then, answering his own question, he said, "No, we're not. So the deal I worked out with Sadler fell through. I still have permission from the Secretary of the Interior to stay here until the seventeenth."

Wolf snickered. So did Warren and one or two of the other Lighthorsemen.

Dillworth glared at them. "What's so funny?"

It was Gabe who answered his question. "That telegraph message you got isn't worth one red cent, Dillworth."

"What the hell are you talking about? It says—"

"I know what it says. It says, as I recall, ' . . . permission is hereby granted for your men and animals to remain in your present location . . . ' and so on."

"That's right, it does."

" 'In your present location,' " Gabe repeated meaningfully. He watched Dillworth start to speak but fail to do so.

He watched the trail boss glance at his men and he saw the understanding flood their eyes as well as Dillworth's.

"Your cattle have moved," Wolf declared. "They're not in their 'present location' anymore. Not now that we've moved them across the river, they're not."

"So you now have absolutely no protection under the edict given in that telegraph message you got from Washington," Gabe pointed out.

"I'll—we'll move them back!" Dillworth blustered.

Gabe shook his head. "No you won't. We won't let you."

"The only place you'll move them," Wolf said, "is north until you're out of Chickasaw Nation altogether."

"Which, in my book, will be good riddance to bad rubbish," Warren added.

"They've got us over a barrel, Boss," Curly told Dillworth. "We've not got a legal leg to stand on anymore."

"Curly's right," Gabe agreed. "So hit the trail, Dillworth."

It took some time to bring the chuck wagon across the river but at last it arrived. When it did, the Lighthorsemen saw to it that it kept right on going—north. Behind it, the young wrangler drove the remuda.

Dillworth and his drovers reluctantly moved out, taking up positions at the head, behind, and on the flanks of the herd. All the Lighthorsemen except Wolf rode along with them, keeping the trail boss and his drovers under their drawn guns.

Gabe held out his hand.

Wolf shook it. "I'm glad you were playing this game on our side, Gabe. If you'd been on Dillworth's side, I'm sure you would have found a way to outwit us. Are you coming with us?"

"Why not? I'd like to see a little more of Chickasaw Nation before I move on."

"Let's go," Wolf said.

He and Gabe moved out, riding together behind the herd as it wended its way north along the Chisholm Trail.

The Horsemen

by Gary McCarthy

The Ballous were the finest horsemen in the South, a Tennessee family famous for the training and breeding of glorious Thoroughbreds. When the Civil War devastated their home and their lives, they headed West—into the heart of Indian territory. As horsemen, they triumphed. As a family, they endured. But as pioneers in a new land, they faced unimaginable hardship, danger, and ruthless enemies. . . .

Turn the page for a preview of this exciting new western series . . .

The Horsemen

Now available from Diamond Books

THE HORSEMEN
by
Gary McCarthy

November 24, 1863—Just east of Chattanooga, Tennessee

The chestnut stallion's head snapped up very suddenly. Its nostrils quivered, then flared, testing the wind, tasting the approach of unseen danger. Old Justin Ballou's watchful eye caught the stallion's motion and he also froze, senses focused. For several long moments, man and stallion remained motionless, and then Justin Ballou opened the gate to the paddock and limped toward the tall Thoroughbred. He reached up and his huge, blue-veined hand stroked the stallion's muzzle. "What is it, High Man?" he asked softly. "What now, my friend?"

In answer, the chestnut dipped its head several times and stamped its feet with increasing nervousness. Justin began to speak soothingly to the stallion, his deep, resonant voice flowing like a mystical incantation. Almost at once, the stallion grew calm. After a few minutes, Justin said, as if to an old and very dear friend, "Is it one of General Grant's Union patrols this time, High Man? Have they come to take what little I have left? If so, I will gladly fight them to the death."

The stallion shook its head, rolled its eyes, and snorted as if it could smell Yankee blood. Justin's thick fingers scratched a special place behind the stallion's ear. The chestnut lowered its head to nuzzle the man's chest.

"Don't worry. It's probably another Confederate patrol," Justin said thoughtfully. "But what can they want this time? I have already given them three fine sons and most of your offspring. There is so little left to give—but they know that! Surely they can see my empty stalls and paddocks."

Justin turned toward the road leading past his neat, whitewashed fences that sectioned and cross-sectioned his famous Tennessee horse ranch, known throughout the South as Wildwood Farm. The paddocks were empty and silent. This cold autumn day, there were proud mares with their colts, and prancing fillies blessed the old man's vision or gave him the joy he'd known for so many years. It was the war—this damned killing Civil War. "No more!" Justin cried. "You'll have no more of my fine horses or sons!"

The stallion spun and galloped away. High Man was seventeen years old, long past his prime, but he and a few other Ballou-bred stallions still sired the fastest and handsomest horses in the South. Just watching the chestnut run made Justin feel a little better. High Man was a living testimony to the extraordinarily fine care he'd received all these years at Wildwood Farms. No one would believe that at his ripe age he could still run and kick his heels up like a three-year-old colt.

The stallion ran with such fluid grace that he seemed to float across the earth. When the Thoroughbred reached the far end of the paddock, it skidded to a sliding stop, chest banging hard against the fence. It spun around, snorted, and shook its head for an expected shout of approval.

But not this day. Instead, Justin made himself leave the paddock, chin up, stride halting but resolute. He could hear thunder growing louder. Could it be the sound of cannon from as far away as the heights that General Bragg and his Rebel army now held in wait of the Union army's expected assault? No, the distance was too great even to carry the roar of heavy artillery. That told Justin that his initial hunch was correct and the sound growing in his ears had to be racing hoofbeats.

But were they enemy or friend? Blue coat or gray? Justin planted his big work boots solidly in the dust of the country road; either way, he would meet them.

"Father!"

He recognized his fourteen-year-old daughter's voice and ignored it, wanting Dixie to stay inside their mansion. Justin drew a pepperbox pistol from his waistband. If this actually was a dreaded Union cavalry patrol, then someone was going to die this afternoon. A man could only be pushed so far and then he had to fight.

"Father!" Dixie's voice was louder now, more strident. "Father!"

Justin reluctantly twisted about to see his daughter and her oldest brother, Houston, running toward him. Both had guns clenched in their fists.

"Who is it!" Houston gasped, reaching Justin first and trying to catch his wind.

Justin did not dignify the stupid question with an answer. In a very few minutes, they would know. "Dixie, go back to the house."

"Please, I . . . I just can't!"

"Dixie! Do as Father says," Houston stormed. "This is no time for arguing. Go to the house!"

Dixie's black eyes sparked. She stood her ground. Houston was twenty-one and a man full grown, but he was still just her big brother. "I'm staying."

Houston's face darkened with anger and his knuckles whitened as he clutched the gun in his fist. "Dammit, you heard . . ."

"Quiet, the both of you!" Justin commanded. "Here they come."

A moment later a dust-shrouded patrol lifted from the earth to come galloping up the road.

"It's *our* boys," Dixie yelped with relief. "It's a Reb patrol!"

"Yeah," Houston said, taking an involuntary step forward, "but they been shot up all to hell!"

Justin slipped his gun back into his waistband and was seized by a flash of dizziness. Dixie moved close, steadying him until the spell passed a moment later. "You all right?"

Justin nodded. He did not know what was causing the dizziness, but the spells seemed to come often these days. No doubt, it was the war. This damned war that the South was steadily losing. And the death of two of his five strapping sons and . . .

Houston had stepped out in front and now he turned to shout, "Mason is riding with them!"

Justin's legs became solid and strong again. Mason was the middle son, the short, serious one that wanted to go into medicine and who read volumes of poetry despite the teasing from his brothers.

Dixie slipped her gun into the pocket of the loose-fitting pants she insisted on wearing around the horses. She glanced up at her father and said, "Mason will be hungry and so will the others. They'll need food and bandaging."

"They'll have both," Justin declared without hesitation, "but no more of my Thoroughbreds!"

"No more," Dixie vowed. "Mason will understand."

"Yeah," Houston said, coming back to stand by his father, "but the trouble is, he isn't in charge. That's a captain he's riding alongside."

Justin was about to speak, but from the corner of his eyes, saw a movement. He twisted, hand instinctively lifting the pepperbox because these woods were crawling with both Union and Confederate deserters, men often half-crazy with fear and hunger.

"Pa, don't you dare shoot me!" Rufus "Ruff" Ballou called, trying to force a smile as he moved forward, long and loose limbed with his rifle swinging at his side.

"Ruff, what the hell you doing hiding in those trees!" Houston demanded, for he too had been startled enough to raise his gun.

If Ruff noticed the heat in his older brother's voice, he chose to ignore it.

"Hell, Houston, I was just hanging back a little to make sure these were friendly visitors."

"It's Mason," Justin said, turning back to the patrol. "And from the looks of these boys, things are going from bad to worse."

There were just six men in the patrol, two officers and four enlisted. One of the enlisted was bent over nearly double with pain, a blossom of red spreading across his left shoulder. Two others were riding double on a runty sorrel.

"That sorrel is gonna drop if it don't get feed and rest," Ruff observed, his voice hardening with disapproval.

"All of their mounts look like they've been chased to hell and back without being fed or watered," Justin stated. "We'll make sure they're watered and grained before these boys leave."

The Ballous nodded. It never occurred to any of them that a horse should ever leave their farm in worse shape then when it had arrived. The welfare of livestock just naturally came first—even over their own physical needs.

Justin stepped forward and raised his hand in greeting. Deciding that none of the horses were in desperate circumstances, he fixed his attention on Mason. He was shocked. Mason was a big man, like his father and brothers, but now he appeared withered—all ridges and angles. His cap was missing and his black hair was wild and unkept. His cheeks were hollow, and the sleeve of his right arm had been cut away, and now his arm was wrapped in a dirty bandage. The loose, sloppy way he sat his horse told Justin more eloquently than words how weak and weary Mason had become after just eight months of fighting the armies of the North.

The patrol slowed to a trot, then a walk, and Justin saw the captain turn to speak to Mason. Justin couldn't hear the words, but he could see by the senior officer's expression that the man was angry and upset. Mason rode trancelike, eyes fixed on his family, lips a thin, hard slash instead of the expected smile of greeting.

Mason drew his horse to a standstill before his father and brothers. Up close, his appearance was even more shocking.

"Mason?" Justin whispered when his son said nothing. "Mason, are you all right?"

Mason blinked. Shook himself. "Father. Houston. Ruff. Dixie. You're all looking well. How are the horses?"

"What we got left are fine," Justin said cautiously. "Only a few on the place even fit to run. Sold all the fillies and colts last fall. But you knew that."

"You did the right thing to keep Houston and Ruff out of this," Mason said.

Houston and Ruff took a sudden interest in the dirt under their feet. The two youngest Ballou brothers had desperately wanted to join the Confederate army, but Justin had demanded that they remain at Wildwood Farm, where they could help carry on the family business of raising Thoroughbreds. Only now, instead of racetracks and cheering bettors, the Ballou horses swiftly carried messages between the generals of the Confederate armies. Many times the delivery of a vital message depended on horses with pure blazing speed.

"Lieutenant," the captain said, clearing his throat loudly, "I think this chatter has gone on quite long enough. Introduce me."

Mason flushed with humiliation. "Father, allow me to introduce Captain Denton."

Justin had already sized up the captain, and what he saw did not please him. Denton was a lean, straight-backed man. He rode as if he had a rod up his ass and he looked like a mannequin glued to the saddle. He was an insult to the fine tradition of Southern cavalry officers.

"Captain," Justin said without warmth, "if you'll order your patrol to dismount, we'll take care of your wounded and these horses."

"Private Wilson can't ride any farther," Denton said. "And there isn't time for rest."

"But you *have* to," Justin argued. "These horses are—"

"Finished," Denton said. "We must have replacements, that's why we are here, Mr. Ballou."

Justin paled ever so slightly. "Hate to tell you this, Captain, but I'm afraid you're going to be disappointed. I've already given all the horses I can to the Confederacy—sons, too."

Denton wasn't listening. His eyes swept across the paddock.

"What about *that* one," he said, pointing toward High Man. "He looks to be in fine condition."

"He's past his racing prime," Houston argued. "He's our foundation sire now and is used strictly for breeding."

"Strictly for breeding?" Denton said cryptically. "Mr. Ballou, there is not a male creature on this earth who would not like to—"

"Watch your tongue, sir!" Justin stormed. "My daughter's honor will not be compromised!"

Captain Denton's eyes jerked sideways to Dixie and he blushed. Obviously, he had not realized Dixie was a girl with her baggy pants and a felt slouch hat pulled down close to her eyebrows. And a Navy Colt hanging from her fist.

"My sincere apologies." The captain dismissed her and his eyes came to rest on the barns. "You've got horses in those stalls?"

"Yes, but—"

"I'd like to see them," Denton said, spurring his own flagging mount forward.

Ruff grabbed his bit. "Hold up there, Captain, you haven't been invited."

"And since when does an officer of the Confederacy need to beg permission for horses so that *your* countrymen, as well as mine, can live according to our own laws!"

"*I'm* the law on this place," Justin thundered. "And my mares are in foal. They're not going to war, Captain. Neither they nor the last of my stallions are going to be chopped to pieces on some battlefield or have their legs ruined while trying to pull supply wagons. These are *Thoroughbred* horses, sir! Horses bred to race."

"The race," Denton said through clenched teeth, "is to see if we can bring relief to our men who are, this very moment, fighting and dying at Lookout Mountain and Missionary Ridge."

Denton's voice shook with passion. "The plundering armies of General Ulysses Grant, General George Thomas, and his Army of the Cumberland are attacking our soldiers right now, and God help me if I've ever seen such slaughter! Our boys are dying, Mr. Ballou! Dying for the right to determine the South's great destiny. We—not you and your piddling horses—are making the ultimate sacrifices! But maybe your attitude has a lot to do with why you married a Cherokee Indian woman."

Something snapped behind Justin Ballou's obsidian eyes. He saw the faces of his two oldest sons, one reported to have been blown to pieces by a Union battery in the battle of Bull Run and the other trampled to death in a bloody charge at Shiloh. Their proud mother's Cherokee blood had made them the first in battle and the first in death.

Justin lunged, liver-spotted hands reaching upward. Too late Captain Denton saw murder in the old man's eyes. He tried to rein his horse off, but Justin's fingers clamped on his coat and his belt. With a tremendous heave, Denton was torn from his saddle and hurled to the ground. Justin growled like a huge dog as his fingers crushed the breath out of Denton's life.

He would have broken the Confederate captain's neck if his sons had not broken his stranglehold. Two of the mounted soldiers reached for their pistols, but Ruff's own rifle made them freeze and then slowly raise their hands.

"Pa!" Mason shouted, pulling Justin off the nearly unconscious officer. "Pa, stop it!"

As suddenly as it had flared, Justin's anger ended, and he had to be helped to his feet. He glared down at the wheezing cavalry officer and his voice trembled when he said, "Captain Denton, I don't know how the hell you managed to get a commission in Jeff Davis's army, but I do know this: lecture me about sacrifice for the South again and I will break your fool neck! Do you hear me!"

The captain's eyes mirrored raw animal fear. "Lieutenant Ballou," he choked at Mason, "I *order* you in the name of the Army of the Confederacy to confiscate fresh horses!"

"Go to hell."

"I'll have you court-martialed and shot for insubordination!"

Houston drew his pistol and aimed it at Denton's forehead. "Maybe you'd better change your tune, Captain."

"No!"

Justin surprised them all by coming to Denton's defense. "If you shoot him—no matter how much he deserves to be shot—our family will be judged traitors."

"But . . ."

"Put the gun away," Justin ordered wearily. "I'll give him fresh horses."

"Pa!" Ruff cried. "What are you going to give to him? Our mares?"

"Yes, but not all of them. Just the youngest and the strongest. And those matched three-year-old stallions you and Houston are training."

"But, Pa," Ruff protested, "they're just green broke."

"I know, but this will season them in a hurry," Justin said levelly. "Besides, there's no choice. High Man leaves Wildwood Farm over my dead body."

"Yes, sir," Ruff said, knowing his father was not running a bluff.

Dixie turned away in anger and started toward the house. "I'll see we get food cooking for the soldiers and some fresh bandages for Private Wilson."

A moment later, Ruff stepped over beside the wounded soldier. "Here, let me give you a hand down. We'll go up to the house and take a look at that shoulder."

Wilson tried to show his appreciation as both Ruff and Houston helped him to dismount. "Much obliged," he whispered. "Sorry to be of trouble."

Mason looked to his father. "Sir, I'll take responsibility for your horses."

"How can you do that?" Houston demanded of his brother. "These three-year-old stallions and our mares will go crazy amid all that cannon and rifle fire. No one but us can control them. It would be—"

"Then you and Ruff need to come on back with us," Mason said.

"No!" Justin raged. "I paid for their replacements! I've got the papers saying that they can't be drafted or taken into the Confederate army."

"Maybe not," Mason said, "but they can volunteer to help us save lives up on the mountains where General Bragg is in danger of being overrun, and where our boys are dying for lack of medical attention."

"No!" Justin choked. "I've given too much already!"

"Pa, we won't fight. We'll just go to handle the horses." Ruff placed his hand on his father's shoulder. "No fighting," he pledged, looking past his father at the road leading toward Chattanooga and the battlefields. "I swear it."

Justin shook his head, not believing a word of it. His eyes shifted from Mason to Houston and finally settled on Ruff. "You boys are *fighters*! Oh, I expect you'll even try to do as you promised, but you won't be able to once you smell gunpowder and death. You'll fight and get yourselves killed, just like Micha and John."

Mason shook his head vigorously. "Pa, I swear that once the horses are delivered and hitched to those ambulances and supply wagons, I'll send Houston and Ruff back to you. All right?"

After a long moment, Justin finally managed to nod his head. "Come along," he said to no one in particular, "we'll get our Thoroughbreds ready."

But Captain Denton's thin lips twisted in anger. "I want a *dozen* horses! Not one less will do. And I still want that big chestnut stallion in that paddock for my personal mount."

Houston scoffed with derision, "Captain, I've seen some fools in my short lifetime, but none as big as you."

"At least," Denton choked, "my daddy didn't buy my way out of the fighting."

Houston's face twisted with fury and his hand went for the Army Colt strapped to his hip. It was all that Ruff could do to keep his older brother from gunning down the ignorant cavalry officer.

"You *are* a fool," Ruff gritted at the captain when he'd calmed Houston down. "And if you should be lucky enough to survive this war, you'd better pray that you never come across me or any of my family."

Denton wanted to say something. His mouth worked but Ruff's eyes told him he wouldn't live long enough to finish even a single sentence, so the captain just clamped his mouth shut and spun away in a trembling rage.

A special offer for people who enjoy reading the best Westerns published today.

WESTERNS!

NO OBLIGATION

Mail the coupon below

To start your subscription and receive 2 FREE WESTERNS, fill out the coupon below and mail it today. We'll send your first shipment which includes 2 FREE BOOKS as soon as we receive it.